Sarah Burton

Sarah Burton is a writer and academic who lectures in Theatre Studies and Creative Writing. She has written and produced five community plays, including the longest-running community play of its kind in Britain.

She is an established author and has written two critically acclaimed books: *A Double Life: A Biography of Charles and Mary Lamb* and *Impostors: Six Kinds of Liar.*

First published in the UK in 2011 by Aurora Metro Press
67 Grove Avenue, Twickenham, Middlesex TW1 4HX
www.aurorametro.com

With thanks to Jonathan Petheridge, Charles Way, Jonas Basom, Amersham
Museum, Anne Burton, Claque Theatre, Robin Emery, Ann Jellicoe, Gina Keene,
Jon Oram, Cathy Priestley, Fiona Reid, Dominic Sharp, Laura Shearing, Isabel
Sheridan, John Shippey, Leslie Stewart, Roy Truman, the creators of the website
tourismnortheast.co.uk and Alice Williams.

Thanks also to Jack Timney, Martin Gilbert, Simon Smith, Lesley Mackay, Jackie
Glasgow, Neil Gregory, Richard Turk, Laurane Marchive, Thomas Skinner,
Sumedha Mane and Jeni Calnan.

Photographs by Beth Ashmeade, Ian Ashmeade, Zoe Ashmeade and Geoff Durrant.

Printed by Ashford Colour Press, Fareham, UK.
ISBN: 978-1-906582-15-9

THEATRE FOR CHILDREN AND YOUNG PEOPLE

ed. Stuart Bennett

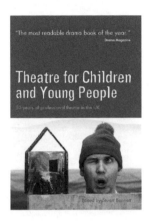

50 years of professional theatre in the UK

The first publication to give the whole story of Theatre for Children and Young People and its development in the UK, this is essential reading for drama and theatre practitioners and for students of contemporary British theatre everywhere.

'Need evidence that theatre is crucial to education? The Association of Children and Young People's Theatre has amassed it in a compilation book which explores developments in the last 50 years.' *The Stage*

'The most readable drama book of the year.' *Drama Magazine*

£11.99
ISBN 0-9546912-8-8
250 pages pbk

www.aurorametro.com

How to put on a Community Play

by

SARAH BURTON

In loving memory of Mary Stewart

(1918–2010)

How to put on a Community Play

by

SARAH BURTON

AURORA METRO PRESS

CONTENTS

●

1. Getting Started

'Our story begins in Jerusalem, in the days of Herod the King...' As the Storyteller's opening lines rang out I could hear he was nervous and my own heart was thumping hard. To be honest, we were all terrified.

Our own story had begun a year earlier, Christmas 2000, when my husband, Leslie, had suggested we put on a Nativity play in our own community (Haddenham in Cambridgeshire). There had been no conventional Nativity at the village school that year and it had set us thinking. What if we put on our own play? What if we avoided the usual clichés – casting adults for the adult parts and using children only to play children? What if we tried to portray Mary and Joseph as real people? What if we included legends as well as the details in the gospels? What if we tried to get the whole village involved?

Fast forward one year and to the end of that first performance: Leslie (who is scared of heights) is unfeasibly high up in a lighting gantry at one end of our village church, while I am at the other end, singing the 'Hallelujah Chorus' with a cast of 180 (a large proportion of whom are children). As soon as it is over, the choir – who are also the crowd – are embracing each other, many of them in tears, but far from unhappy. Gina, the wardrobe mistress, hugs me and later reports that I said in her ear: 'I think we got away with it.' In fact, I am relieved mainly that nobody died.

Many of the audience members are also showing signs of emotion. Our butcher, far from dry-eyed himself, gives me a hug (he has never given me a hug before) and says: 'I'm not religious, but that really *meant* something.' Other people, that night, and over the ensuing days, testify to the great success of the experiment, and seem to be awed in equal measure by the standard of the theatrical experience and by the fact that it was all done in *our* village, by *us*.

Our first community play – the 'one-off' Nativity – proved a great success in every sense except its 'one-offness'. The community took it to its heart and it is now an established local tradition. Since 2001, we have mounted a production every two years. But the first time it was new to everybody and much more like a community play project will be for most people. Most of the experience and advice I am sharing in this book are lessons we learnt the hard way during the first production; others are the result of having had the opportunity to refine and experiment on subsequent occasions. In other words, this is the book I wish I had had at my side ten years ago.

The purpose of this book

Books on community plays do exist, but all those I have found are out of date, out of print, or focus on the subject entirely from an academic perspective. (This is because there has been a phenomenal growth in academic interest in the subject, and it is now included on an increasing number of university Theatre Studies courses.) It is notoriously unwise to attempt to predict cultural and economic trends, but there are factors quite outside our own preoccupations as community play-makers which may well benefit the form in the foreseeable future.

There is every reason to suggest that the community play is ripe for a revival over the next few years. Principally, changes in arts funding may well produce a climate in which – to anyone thinking creatively at least – the community play could increasingly be seen as an 'answer'. As we all know, local arts funding has been slashed across the country and will no doubt be squeezed for the foreseeable future. At the same time, and independently of this fact, much of the emphasis on arts funding has for a while now been placed on broadening appeal and widening access to the arts.

Community plays ideally accommodate both these factors, providing an extremely cost-efficient way for funders to fulfil their 'outreach' criteria. Arts bodies are more willing to fund professional writers and directors to go into a community to create a play with local people, as well as plays which spring spontaneously from those communities themselves. This is because the voluntary (unpaid) input from the community more than matches the value of this funding, with generally spectacular results. Everyone (including the funder) benefits. Another aspect of the almost guaranteed success of the community play is that there is essentially a large local captive audience with direct or indirect links to the production. The interest and support of local businesses (including local media) and other local organisations is a further advantage which professional productions can't always depend upon. Given all these factors, there is every reason to believe we could see a strong rise in community theatre and support for it.

Considering that arts funding has been under pressure for many years now,

and the proven artistic and community benefits of these enterprises, it seems surprising that there are not more community plays already. I believe that this is because such a project, while a very attractive idea, is a thoroughly daunting prospect given that there seems to be no readily available advice or guidance on how you even begin to go about it. Intrepid pioneers find their own bruising and bloody way, and though triumphant and exhilarating in the event, the process is often too exhausting to desire ever to attempt it again. To give a vivid personal example, I lost one and-a-half stone in weight in four months in the lead-up to our first community play (and I only weighed eight stone to begin with).

Finally, although I have a Ph.D. in Theatre Studies, only doing a community play could have prepared me for doing a community play. So while I hope you find the following pages useful and helpful, some of the guidance may not be relevant to your specific situation, as all community plays are unique. Only you know your community and your play. While this book attempts to be a comprehensive guide, it's not a foolproof manual. If it saves you unnecessary time and trouble, it will have done its job.

Theatre is always an organic collaborative process, as the production

develops and changes shape throughout the rehearsal period. This is even more true of the community play, due to its provisional nature. Aspects of the play are more likely to have to be rethought due to additional practical considerations. Areas overlap and a development in one can have an impact on another. Much of the advice and many of the tips this book contains are the result of personal experience and I will illustrate many of the points with incidents from my own engagement with community theatre as a way of making concrete examples of what might otherwise seem unhelpfully theoretical. I have generally organised the material into sections where I first describe a particular aspect of the production in general (i.e.. of *any* production) and then add, by way of illustration, how we addressed or approached it in the context of our own community play.

Defining the community play

What is a community play? Let's begin with two different groups' views. Dorchester Community Play Association usefully defines it thus:

> The essence of the modern community play is that it tells a story taken from the community's past. Typically, the historical setting will be factual while the actual story may be fictitious but nevertheless makes use of authentic material. And if the play has resonances today so much the better. The whole purpose of a community play is to draw together the local community and to involve as many people as possible in all its varying aspects including, of course, those who come simply to watch and enjoy the finished work. Thus a good community play is one which not only earns accolades for the quality of its performance but succeeds also in uniting the community in a common artistic enterprise.

> The community play is open to all. It is not just about acting or singing, although there is plenty of both, but about everything which precedes them, the research which goes into the play writing, the workshops, the costume making, the stage design, the props, the sound and lighting, the stage management and all the numerous front of house activities. There can be few people who don't have something to offer among all these different activities. Participation in the play is a wonderful way of making friends and finding out more about other people and about yourself. Many of us have hidden talents and abilities which the play draws out to everyone's surprise including our own.

It has been the practice in Dorchester to employ a professional director and designer. Not only has this helped achieve a high quality of production, it has enabled ordinary people to learn professional skills.

Woking Community Play Association defines it as follows:

A community play is a celebration. It is specially written or created for a particular town, capturing within it something of the essence of that place. It requires considerable numbers of enthusiastic individuals to work together on a large scale project that is developed over a long period.

A community play is directed by a small team of professionals who work in collaboration with local people to enable the play to be creative, artistically successful and to achieve the highest possible standards. Their expertise ensures efficient organisation and provides a framework for the potential of local enthusiasts to be explored and given full rein.

A community play is above all about people; about making friends, learning new skills, gaining confidence and breaking down barriers.

It actively engages people of all ages, backgrounds and abilities to work together creatively. A project of this kind has something to offer everyone.

It introduces people, many uninitiated, to theatre art forms creating a sense of community spirit and a local identity for all involved.

It aims to touch, in some way, thousands of people as participants, as members of the audience, within fund raising activities, through direct and indirect involvement.

It is an opportunity for wide ranging links to be made within a community, between individuals and organisations.

It is a firm foundation on which to build many future activities both for individuals and groups.

These two definitions, which broadly agree, are cited because of the clarity of their objectives. Both view a high standard of performance as absolutely reconcilable with the recruitment of inexperienced participants. The social benefits – for social cohesion and for individual growth – are important outcomes for both groups.

Dorchester Community Play Association is a well-established organisation with a number of productions under its belt; Woking Community Play Association was set up for one big production, but continues to exist creating smaller events. Both received substantial public funding (Dorchester CPA's last production cost over £72,000) and they both pay professionals to initiate and run the project. However, community plays do *not* have to depend either on outside funding or on employing professionals (the two, for obvious reasons, do tend to go hand-in-hand).

Both of these organisations see the community play as indivisible from the subject being a local story, but not all community plays adhere to this. The St. Ives Community Play chose to produce a play by Shakespeare in 2010, and other groups look to the classics for a project around which they can gather and create something that is still uniquely their own. What both Dorchester and Woking implicitly suggest is not that the community play *creates* a community; rather, it is an opportunity to discover what was there all along,

but largely unacknowledged and untested: a community that can work effectively, harmoniously and creatively together, made up of individuals who all have some form of creative potential. What the community play does, is to remind us that there *is* a community, and that what a community can achieve together has unique value precisely because *only* a community can achieve it.

A brief history of the community play

Anyone embarking on a community play is participating in one of the very oldest forms of theatre. The first known plays in the English language were community plays – plays put on *by* local people *for* a local audience. These plays had taken the themes of the liturgical dramas (performed in abbeys and monasteries, mostly in Latin), into the streets of their towns and cities, transforming Biblical figures into three dimensional characters, who spoke the same language as their audience. Crucially, the actors were not professionals; the parts were played by ordinary working people who chose to devote considerable time and resources to putting on a play for their community.

The early community plays, often known as Miracle, Mystery or Cycle plays, were extremely versatile. They required little or no scenery or props and no raised stage, and could be performed in inns or their courtyards, in the halls of private households or in the marketplace. In many cases they were even more mobile. Succeeding scenes (each of which formed a short play in itself) depicting the life of Christ, or the whole Biblical story, from the Creation to the Last Judgement, were presented on wagons, which moved through the town, stopping to perform at designated locations. A complete mystery play (or 'cycle' of playlets) would last for several hours, and was typically repeated over three days, enabling as many of the people from the town and outlying districts to see it as possible.

Stage directions in surviving manuscripts show how effective use was made of simple staging strategies. Props were kept to a minimum of often symbolic items, and much use was made of mime. For example, in the Chester version of *Noah's Flood*, following Noah's family's description of how they are going to help make the Ark, comes the instruction: *Then they make signs as if they were working with different tools.* Location was also simply and clearly suggested. In the same play, just before Noah's family list the animals in the Ark, the staging note reads: *The Ark must be boarded round about, and on the boards all the beasts and fowls hereafter rehearsed must be painted, that these words may agree with the pictures.* Later on, the technical difficulty of showing the dove leaving and returning with evidence that there is dry land is cunningly resolved: *Then he [Noah] shall send forth a dove; and there shall be in the ship another dove bearing an olive branch in her mouth, which Noah shall let down from the mast by a cord in his hand.*

Making do with the available performance space was also clearly part and parcel of the enterprise, as the opening stage direction of the Noah play suggests: *And first in some high place, or in the clouds if it may be, God speaketh unto Noah standing without the Ark with all his family.* In the hall of a large house, God might speak from the minstrel's gallery; in the courtyard of an inn from a balcony, perhaps, while 'clouds' were clearly desirable but not absolutely necessary. This accommodating adaptability is typical of the genre: there is nothing which cannot be achieved or resolved by a willingness to improvise.

While Mystery plays clearly had moral messages, they were by no means exclusively sober affairs, and much use was made of humour. Extra-biblical details from medieval legend found their way into the plays, such as Noah's comically stubborn wife flatly refusing to board the Ark. These touches helped animate Biblical figures as real people, and encouraged the audience to identify with them. Similarly, when the play-makers were faced with fleshing out characters about whom the Bible told them nothing, they had to speculate on how they might have responded to the situation. In the Chester version of *Noah's Flood*, the audience had barely finished laughing at Noah's wife's intransigence when this refusal was revealed as proceeding from a terrible dilemma, as she pleaded with Noah to let her fetch her 'gossips' (female friends and neighbours) as she felt she could not save herself and leave them to drown. The plays are full of such humanising nuances, as when plays dealing with the birth of Christ follow apocryphal legends rather than the gospels in engaging with what many of us have at some point wondered: what Joseph must 'really' have thought about that mysterious pregnancy. Mystery plays literally brought the Bible to life, filling in the gaps where necessary or desirable and infusing it with familiar mortal preoccupations.

A well-known example of comedy introduced purely for its own sake is in the playlet known as *The Wakefield Second Shepherds' Pageant*, in which the tale of a stolen sheep, disguised by the thief and his wife as their baby, is borrowed from folklore and interwoven with the Nativity story. The first lines of the play (in which a shepherd complains about the cold, taxation, and general oppression), tell us more about the shepherds as people than we ever learn from St Luke and pave the way for a story which is by turns funny and moving. The deployment of humour, as well as creative guesswork, on the part of the play-makers, helped the stories along, enabling and encouraging audiences to invest emotionally in the unfolding action.

So a certain realism in characterisation and symbolism in staging combined to assist the play-makers in communicating and engaging with the audience. It is realistic to suppose that the majority of the audience would have been largely familiar with the narratives unfolding before them, which would have had self-evident advantages, yet this was far from universally the case. In a largely pre-literate society, most people's knowledge of the Bible derived from what they heard in Church, and from oral tradition, but not everyone, by any means, attended church, and those that did, did not necessarily take on board the messages being transmitted. Barry Reay's survey of popular religion in the 17th century – several centuries into the miracle play tradition – uncovered evidence of widespread ignorance of the most basic tenets of the Christian church. The extent of this lack of awareness was regarded even at the time, as 'incredible and inconceivable' and Reay cites many examples, one of which is extremely pertinent to our subject:

> An old man from Cartmel, also a regular church attender, did not know how many gods there were. When Christ was mentioned by his questioner he said: 'I think I heard of that man you spoke of, once in a play at Kendall, called Corpus Christi play, where there was a man on a tree, and blood ran down.'

For the old man from Cartmel the enduring and affecting image of Christ's suffering at the crucifixion had nothing to do with the church he had faithfully attended, or the scripture to which he had repeatedly given ear, but was vividly associated with the play he had seen.

So the Mystery plays had an educational function as well, and made sense

to spectators to whom their stories were new, as well as to those familiar with their Scripture. Their role was clearly an important one, as municipal authorities took overall charge of the whole cycle, while the individual plays or pageants were assigned to various guilds. The job of financing and producing the play cycle was thus delegated to a number of smaller groups, each of which would have taken particular pains with their own play, because as far as possible the plays were associated in some way with their own trade and provided an opportunity to advertise their skills.

As well as taking a professional pride in their part of the pageant (and there was presumably some degree of competition between the guilds), putting on the play gave people who worked together the opportunity to do something that *wasn't work* together, while still aiming at the highest possible standard of production. The water-carriers got the opportunity to paint animals on the Ark (the painters of course were busy with the crucifixion), while the tanners had to contrive a tree of knowledge and a serpent for the Fall. Others were required as actors and musicians, as music generally played a significant part in enhancing the drama.

Mystery plays were at their most popular across Europe from the eleventh to the end of the 14th century. However, as late as 1857 Thomas Shaw was able to observe that 'in the pastoral and remote corners' of the continent, 'in the retired valleys of Catholic Switzerland, in the Tyrol, and in some little visited districts of Germany, the peasants still annually perform dramatic spectacles representing episodes in the life of Christ.' The example of this which famously survives to this day is that of Oberammergau, where the local community has mounted such a play, on a spectacular scale, every ten years since 1634. (In the most recent production, involving 2,000 villagers – half the population – Jesus was played by a psychologist and Mary Magdalene by a flight attendant.)

As the religious character of England changed, Mystery plays gradually gave way to Morality plays, popular from the beginning of the 15th century, and Biblical characters were replaced by those which personified vices and virtues (such as Avarice and Mercy), which had to be negotiated by an individual representing all individuals (such as Everyman or Mankind). Over time the Morality play in turn was modified and shortened into the Interlude, a form suited to indoor performance, to a timescale, by professional actors, before the Interlude itself was adapted into the Elizabethan drama as we know it. The glory days of the sprawling populous pageants of the Mysteries were over; plays and playing had become professionalised, the role of the community exiled to that of spectator, rather than participant.

This brief history of the early community play serves not only to demonstrate that it has a long and rich tradition as a culturally and socially enriching form of recreation, but to emphasise that the idea of the play, and the willingness to make the play, go hand-in-hand with the assumption that any practical problem can and will be surmounted by improvisation. If the stories requiring dramatisation contained non-characters, speculation and imagination built them into convincing personalities. Ingenuity and creativity in staging – whether by putting God on a balcony, painting animals on the side of the Ark, or covertly providing Noah with a second dove – confidently offered by the players, were willingly accepted by the spectators. Simple, strong ideas have traditionally provided inexpensive and effective solutions in community theatre.

The success of community theatre in our own time continues to depend on similar strategies. The extraordinarily ambitious scope of the mystery plays was made possible by small groups working together with a common interest to play their part in a vast project, and this combination of co-operative efforts remains key. I have deliberately used the terms play-making and play-makers to emphasise the sense in which these plays were collaborative affairs. We often forget that even the term 'playwright' refers not to a *writer*, but to a *maker* of plays, just as a wheelwright is a maker of wheels. The finished product as it appears to the spectator is never the be-all and end-all of community theatre. The collective act or experience of making the play transforms every individual participant, from prop-maker to player, into a problem-solver and a playwright.

Initiating the play

Sometimes the idea and impetus comes from *within the community* itself. A self-appointed individual, or a small group of like-minded people may then generate local interest (and form a Community Play Association – hereafter CPA). They may or may not choose to bring on board local authority or

national arts advice and funding. On other occasions, the impetus may come from *outside the community*, more than likely *from* a local authority arts funded organisation or department, which seeks to offer a community the opportunity to put on a play. The character of these two types of play can be very different as a result of this, and each has its own unique advantages.

The *inside/out* approach leaves most of the control of the project in the community; if funding is secured on the basis of the CPA's proposal, it will come without strings (other than assurances made by the CPA in its funding application), and the vision and compass of the production will remain with its initiators and participants. The *outside/in* approach will bring funding and expertise with it. A local authority initiating a community play will almost certainly bring in professionals (often from outside the area), and will, to a certain extent, impose its vision and structure on the play. Each of these approaches has its advantages and disadvantages. A disadvantage of the *inside/out* approach may be a lack of professionalism; whereas a disadvantage of the *outside/in* approach may be an excess of bureaucracy. Neither of these outcomes is inevitable and others are possible. A community-led project will find it harder to get things done which involve council co-operation, whereas a local government funded arts organisation already has relationships with other arms of local government. On the other hand, a community led project already has numerous ties, links and relationships which are more difficult for outsiders to establish. Outsiders are likely to be 'judged' by a community and, if inspirational, will earn its respect, admiration and co-operation. Or they may be resented, especially if they appear to have come in 'to show us how to do it', and especially if there is similar talent on the ground already.

Long before we thought of putting on our own community play, I went to see one not far away, which some people in our village, amongst many others, were involved with. I was dismayed at the vast resources which had been expended to a very disappointing result. The subject happened to be an area of local history of which many local people had a thorough knowledge. There were basic errors of historical fact (by the London writer/director) which immediately offended them. Although many local people were involved and participated (some with gusto), the overall look and feel of the production was somehow empty and directionless; it looked like a play which had been put together by a committee. Despite the tens of thousands which had been spent on it, and the professional assistance behind it, the sound was poor, and the lighting unimaginative and not always even competent. It felt like a show by a vast amateur dramatics company that wasn't quite ready for its first night.

Other community plays which bring in professional help fare much better, and there are a number of skilled individuals and professional theatre organisations which specialise in going into communities to help them make their own play – or make a play their own. In the end, it comes down to the quality of the professional input and the interpersonal and diplomatic skills of those employed as to how successful such interventions can be. From my research, it is clear that only very special, talented and charismatic people are able to enter a community and drive its people to tell their story, and much money is wasted (and hopes dashed) by appointing people who tick the right boxes, rather than finding local people uniquely suited to the role, whose qualities may not even register in local authority generated criteria.

Another aspect of the initiative and support for the project coming from outside the community is that it can be politically motivated. A subsequent chapter will cover the many social benefits of the community play, and it is precisely because of these benefits (to social inclusion and cohesion, as well as to individual growth and development) that a council may decide that a particularly run-down urban estate, for example, might be a ripe case for a community play. While such social interventions are often extremely successful, with positive lasting consequences for a community, others may appear patronising, become fraught with problems, and inevitably lead to conflict rather than cohesion.

Theatre for social harmony

Let's first consider a positive example of a community play which was used to promote social harmony in almost unimaginably difficult circumstances. The end of the Second World War saw millions of refugees in displaced persons camps in various parts of Europe. Social historian Fiona Reid writes:

> Among them were forced labourers from the occupied territories, concentration camp survivors, 'racially pure' children who had been kidnapped as breeding material, and women who had been brought in to work in German brothels. There were also the Volksdeutsche – German-speaking peoples from eastern Europe who had initially been welcomed into the Reich – plus Cossacks, Ukrainians and Balts, some of whom had been so oppressed by Stalin that they had chosen to serve under Hitler.

Understandably, tensions ran high in the DP camps. Many of the people working in them were Quakers serving in the Friends' Relief Service and, at Christmas in 1946, they organised Nativity plays in a number of camps, with the aim of binding all the different nationalities together, and they also involved the local German population. Reid observes that the character of the story itself also had particularly poignant meaning for the DPs: 'The Christmas story is one of homelessness, fear, oppression and, ultimately, hope. It was an ideal vehicle for the articulation of DP grief.' While the casting had to be carefully managed (the Virgin Mary had to be played by a Quaker, to avoid 'the hysterical jealousy which the choice of a DP or a German would cause'), in the event the play provided a rare space in which peace and harmony reigned, with no hint of the usual friction and antagonism between the participating groups; as one participant observed: 'Nationalities were forgotten.'

The example of the DP nativities of 1946 show that the community play can be a powerful social tool – perhaps most powerful when the community is fractured. The choice of the play offered Protestant, Catholic and Orthodox Christians a theme around which they could unite (though one wonders how any Jews or Muslims were made to feel included), and the careful stewardship of the non-conformist Quakers was vital to the success of the enterprise.

There is a flip-side to the power of the community play that is organised by 'outsiders', however. The 'community' in the DP camps was a transient one, where daily life was improvised. The camps had not been 'designed' but were put together ad hoc to meet temporary needs. But what is the role of the community play when it is brought into an environment which is designed to be both oppressive and permanent, where punishment is part of the agenda? How does it fit into a location such as a prison or young offenders' unit?

Due to its many social and personal (as well as artistic) benefits, theatre has been deployed in prisons in both the UK and the USA, but not without causing some unease for practitioners. Can prison theatre really express the issues facing prisoners without becoming a vehicle of dissent which makes the drama too hot too handle? (One experiment in the USA, where the prisoners – supervised by theatre practitioners – wrote and performed their own play, ended in riots.) On the other hand, Michael Balfour, in his book *Theatre in Prison* has warned of 'the danger of aligning art too closely with "the system" (even one that attempts to be benign)'. In the context of prison, the 'humanising' function of theatre will never be a fundamental priority. Theatre in prisons therefore 'exists in contradiction to the administrative task of the institution. Prison is in the business of containment, observation, punishment, categorisation, restriction,

separation, and on occasion rehabilitation... So prison theatre, theatre in prisons, is a term in eternal contradiction with itself.'

I give the example of community theatre in prison to outline in an extreme example problems attendant on the outside/in approach. If you are making a play in an environment which has a lot of social problems (let's return to the example of the run-down urban estate), to what extent do you (the facilitator) marshall the moral dimensions of the play? What if the message of the play turns out to be a bleak one? Do you have a responsibility to promote the idea of hope? Does your play actually improve (albeit temporarily) the lives of its community, or is it merely a fleeting distraction from its underlying problems? Is it cement or wallpaper?

Finally, the community play which is initiated outside the community risks not only being sucked into an overtly political/establishment agenda, but being perceived as – horror of horrors – deeply patronizing. Journalist Shirley Dent warns of the danger of officially endorsing and formally organising community arts, which at its worst becomes 'a cloyingly patronising exercise in social engineering'. Community theatre, in this analysis, when initiated, funded and marshalled by government departments, is not community theatre at all, but the sort of theatre the powers that be have decided that community should have. It lacks both spontaneity and authenticity. 'Wherever it is,' Dent concludes, 'community art should be risky and unpredictable and come from people grouping themselves together – not from policy on high.'

While there is much to sympathise with here, just as some communities lack swimming pools and parks, others lack libraries and theatres, and arts organisations which did nothing to amend and address the absence of arts opportunities in these areas would exist merely to serve those who are already well-educated, well-resourced and generally well provided for in terms of access to the arts. It is clear, however, that any arts initiative which comes from outside the community must strenuously avoid a patronizing brief. Apart from anything else, it is doomed to failure.

So, the community play which is originated outside the community has to be very carefully thought out, in quite different ways from the play which springs from the community itself, and an awareness of political, moral and social dimensions, as well as artistic ones, is necessary.

2. Getting Funded

As mentioned in the previous section, a community play initiated and sponsored by a local authority will bring funding with it. If not, you will have to raise or find the funds yourselves. (The 'you' to whom the book is addressed will from here on shift according to the role under discussion.) Chapter 3 will deal with setting up a core team, but at the same time – if not earlier – you will have to start budgeting and fundraising.

Begin by identifying who is going to be in charge of the budget, and who is going to be responsible for fundraising. These are ideally (a) the same person or (b) two people who can work well together. You do not want either to be someone who is hard to get hold of, when you need a quick decision or piece of information. Your fundraiser needs to have good communication and organisational skills, excellent written English, a very good knowledge of the project, the ability to think creatively, a healthy balance of optimism and realism and lots of common sense. They also need to be aware that they are absolutely crucial to the project – without funds there will be no play, so don't choose anyone you doubt is up to the job. They may also feel the weight of this responsibility, so make sure they are well supported and encourage them to delegate where possible. (For example, anyone can stuff 100 envelopes – the fundraiser can be using his or her time more effectively.) If you have enough people, a fundraising support group is ideal.

The first thing you will need to do is open a bank account in the name of your newly formed organisation. Many funders require that this account must have two signatories for cheques, and it will save a lot of time if the person in charge of the budget is one of these. Assign two other potential signatories (so you can get hold of one if not the other – again avoid people who may be hard to contact in a hurry – e.g. people who work away from home, travel a lot). Funders will also want to know you have got (and might want to see) a constitution. (See advice on this, and a model constitution you can use or adapt in Chapter 7.) In the constitution you will state the major officers in your organisation. Again, it may save time if your Treasurer is also your fundraiser.

Because your community play will aim to reach outside the usual theatre-going demographic, you will be aiming to keep your ticket prices as low as possible. Start thinking about this now and calculate what the likely numbers of spectators will be over all the performances and hence how much you will raise from ticket sales. If you begin with a minimum and see later on that you are going to fall short financially, you can always revise ticket prices upwards, or better still, have two tiers of prices, one budget, and one more expensive, but with some superior value. Another approach is to have your last night as a gala night, where tickets are substantially more expensive. As the last night is often the most subscribed, this can raise quite a bit. However, tickets are not going to cover your costs, by any means, so you have got to think about other sources of funding.

Now you have to work out what it is all going to cost. You may wish to operate your play on the basis that no participant (including the director and producer) is paid for their *time*; and only pay for services which you cannot provide yourselves. You will need to negotiate with the writer whether a fee will be paid by the CPA or whether the writing of the playscript will be unpaid.

Think about your principal costs first and get estimates from the people the producer and director have in mind. Hopefully, the producer or director will already have approached them and they will understand that this is a community project and may be prepared to shave their price down (especially if a local company).

You need a budget for:

Expenditure:

- script (if you are paying a writer or acquiring performing rights)

- music (if you are paying a composer or using copyright music)

- venue – rental for rehearsals and performances. (You may be able to negotiate these for nothing, or for a nominal fee, especially if the organisation involved has a link to your project)

- set construction

- lighting

- sound

- costumes

- props

- administrative costs (If you think these will be low you will be surprised.) Photocopying bills alone can be huge. Don't forget the cost of copying a large number of scripts, as well as music; copying schedules and updates for the cast; copying posters and programmes.)

- insurance

- publicity

- contingency/unforeseen expenses

Income:

- ticket sales

Add 5-10% to your total for contingency, then subtract your projected income from ticket sales – this is the sum you have to raise. You are certain to be in four or five figures now – this is a lot of money and you need to get cracking straight away as it will take any organisation, whether one you approach for a grant or one you approach for sponsorship, a while to process your application.

If you are faced with a sum you think is impossible to raise, go back to your big costs and see whether the people concerned are prepared to pare them down. Although you should generally comport yourself as though the play is inevitable, to *these* people you *can* suggest that the costs could make the project unfeasible and that the whole thing is in jeopardy – they are then faced with a choice between taking a smaller profit, or having no job at all from you.

Look at each cost on its own. Take costumes, for example: with costume hire you may well be in a position to negotiate downwards. If the costumes you need are unlikely to be in huge demand, your costume hirer may be prepared to let you have things at a reduced rate, rather than not be able to hire anything at all to you. Offer them free advertising, or a prominent acknowledgement as a sponsor. Offering to pay in advance may well get you a discount (though don't do this, of course, unless you are certain the production is going ahead).

Consider photocopying: is there an organisation which is either involved or sympathetic which would let you use their facilities free of charge – or just at paper and ink cost? If using a company to do your copying, would they consider being advertised as a major sponsor in return for doing a fixed amount of copying for nothing? Look at set building, lighting and sound – a lot of the costs are labour costs – can you provide volunteers to hump equipment in and out of the venue? Can you provide a volunteer lighting or sound assistant? Can you provide equipment transport? Look again at your venue costs – is there somewhere else, less ideal, where you can rehearse for nothing, or for a donation towards lighting and heating? Look at your publicity costs – can you get volunteers to do a saturation leaflet drop in your target area, rather than pay for advertisements? Present your case to the producer and director and make sure you all understand the need to revise the budget, and get them to help you identify the areas where cuts will have the least impact. There may be production costs which seem extravagant to you, but may be an essential part of their vision for the play. Try to make sure there is an understanding that there will have to be compromises and get them to address what they could manage without. (There are some costs which are irreducible, such as insurance.)

You need to work closely with the production team generally, and avoid a 'them' and 'us' situation, where you are laying down the law on the budget and they are fighting for the things they want. Keep them abreast of developments so there are no nasty shocks – inform them of good news as well as bad. However, remain upbeat – no-one needs a prophet of doom haunting the production – and do recruit help if you find it is all getting too much. Not only another pair of hands but another pair of eyes is always useful.

Sources of money

The main sources of funding are:

Local authorities.

The Arts Councils of England, Scotland, Northern Ireland and Wales.

Lottery funders.

Trusts: Grant-making trusts and foundations provide funding for charitable purposes from returns on investments made by trustees. Trusts need to convince the Inland Revenue that they use their income only for charitable purposes and so may only be able to help if your group is already a charity.

Companies: national and local.

Other organisations: schools, churches, rotary clubs, other community groups. These may be able to give or lend you things you might otherwise have to pay for, if not a financial contribution.

Individuals.

Arts and lottery organisations

Arts and lottery organisations should be your first port of call. Every organisation has its own criteria for funding and its own application process, and the first thing to do is to study these closely. When looking at their funding criteria, note the boxes that your project ticks. The points where their criteria and your project match are the cornerstones of your case and these are the things to emphasise in your application. Look at the process from the funders' point of view: they have limited funds which it is their job to distribute – they also have to be able to justify their decision – so you have to make it as easy as possible for them to say 'yes'. You need your application to be reassuring as well as informative. The budget must look realistic, the organisation must appear competent, the projected outcomes must seem feasible.

Your director and producer will have clear ideas about what they want to achieve and how they are going to achieve it, but this needs to be translated into funders' terms. Together with the director and producer you need to formally express, in clear language, your *aims*, *objectives* and *methods* – these are keywords. Aims and objectives are often confused, but *aims* are the changes you hope to achieve as a result of your work whereas *objectives* are the activities you will undertake and the services you will offer to bring these changes about. So identifying your *aims* means projecting your organisation to the day after your production has finished: what has it achieved that wasn't there before? These will be the social and artistic benefits. Defining your *objectives* means returning to where you are now and explaining through which activities these goals will be achieved. Again, this can seem to overlap with *methods*, so you could confine *methods* to a description of how you are going to deliver your *objectives*.

If this is confusing you already, here is a concrete example of aims, objectives and methods for an imaginary community play:

Aims, objectives and methods of Ourtown Community Play Association

Aims [what you want to achieve in broad strokes]

The OCPA exists to promote and develop community theatre in Ourtown and surrounding areas, with strong emphasis on its proven social as well as artistic benefits.

Objectives [a more developed and specific remit]

To mount a large scale, open access community play of the highest possible standard, framed around the revolt at the Ourtown Union Workhouse in 1880.

To promote social cohesion.

To enhance the opportunities for personal development (by building both skills and confidence).

To celebrate our community's history.

To develop a culture of pride in what we are able to achieve by working together as a community.

Methods

Having recruited a cast which represents all sectors of the community, and having secured the co-operation and participation of existing community groups and organisations (such as Ourtown School, Ourtown Singers and Ourtown Community Centre) the OCPA will recruit experienced and qualified practitioners who will help participants explore and develop theatrical, musical and technical skills, through regular and

structured workshops and rehearsals leading up to the performances. Every effort will be made to attract an audience, as well as a cast and production crew, from parts of the community not historically involved with theatre. The production itself will offer the citizens of Ourtown (which has no permanent theatre) a unique opportunity to see a production of a professional standard at an eminently affordable price.

There will be things you want to say in favour of your project which will make your aims, objectives and methods too lengthy (especially if you have to fit them in a box on the form, or your number of words is limited). Keep a note of these, as forms often ask you for additional information in support of your application, and you can attach extra sheets. Additional information can include the support you have of any 'names' – ideally get a well-known local person or a well-known actor to write you a letter supporting your initiative and testifying to the ability of the director or producer or writer, which you can include in your submission. (They can give their 'wholehearted support to this exciting and worthwhile enterprise' without lifting a finger other than writing the letter – so pull any strings you can to secure this kind of endorsement.) Written support from the local head teacher, the vicar, the mayor, even your M.P. or anyone else you can think of, all help your project look well supported. Also include any press clippings or reviews of similar projects the key organizers may have been instrumental in. (Send copies of everything you enclose and never originals – you may well need them again for another application.)

Ask people to write not just of the desirability of your project, but the *need* for it and the idea of *need* is something you should focus on too. When looking at what the play can offer your community in social terms, focus on the things your community *lacks*. How far away is the nearest professional theatre? How good is the public transport system connecting your community to it? (If it is a distance and the buses etc. are few and far between, this is a plus for you, as there is an identifiable need for your project.) Is there plenty for young people to do in the evenings in your area? If not, then this too is an advantage for you – again your project answers a tangible need. Are there local opportunities for people interested in music or drama to participate free of charge? The answer is likely to be no. Even subsidised evening classes are expensive and choirs and amateur theatre groups often require quite hefty termly or annual subscriptions – or a weekly charge. This is in your favour: you are offering an activity which is open to every member of the community, regardless of their ability to pay: you are meeting a concrete need. (Include statistical support for your case wherever possible.) Although arts organisations who offer funding often include social criteria, non-arts organisations will be particularly interested in the social functions of your project. If your project seems to them to meet real needs in the community, you are in with as good a chance as anybody else.

Having identified the sources whose funding criteria your project fits, you might target particular parts of the budget on particular organisations. There may be a special grant for children's activities, for example. In your budget you are unlikely to have costed children's involvement separately, but you can calculate a proportion of your overall costs and break this up into costs of rehearsal time, adult supervision and coaching, costumes, administration, etc. In the application to this organisation you would then focus on the benefits exclusively to children of being involved in the production. Similarly, you could approach a music fund for assistance in funding your scratch choir or orchestra. Generally you ought not to pin all your hopes on one source of funding, but to spread your funding base as widely as you can.

Before you sit down to make an application, telephone the organisation to make absolutely sure that yours is the kind of event which meets their criteria and to check the deadline. In these uncertain times you may discover that the budget for this period is already spent, that the grant has ceased to be available, or that the funding criteria have changed. Filling in forms and providing supporting material takes time and you need to be sure yours is not wasted making inappropriate applications.

Finding a key

Now you need to play 'snap' with these criteria. Phrases which the community play fundraiser can latch onto include support offered for: 'activities that help arts organisations'; 'investment in ideas, in talent, in education, in places'; 'promoting the value and importance of the arts to everyone'; 'developing high quality arts activity'; 'improving local communities and the lives of people most in need'; 'improving opportunities for people to take part in arts and community activities'; 'helping communities to meet their needs through voluntary action, self-help projects, local facilities or events'; 'extending access and participation'; 'increasing skill and creativity'; 'activities which help to develop people and organisations, improve skills and raise standards'; 'projects which involve people in their communities.'

'Improving the quality of life' is certainly a claim the community play can make, though it is a tricky one to pin down, but the fact that involvement in this kind of activity can improve health and welfare is one you can also promote, using the evidence provided later in this section.

So you've played 'snap' and made a list of where their criteria overlaps

with your aspirations. The next thing to do is to make absolutely certain that your project qualifies, in principle, for funding. Study their criteria and any exclusions. There is no point trying to dress up your project as something it's not. If you are at all unsure, telephone them and ask. (They are quite used to this and used to dealing with people who are doing this for the first time and will be helpful.)

Make a few copies of the (blank) application form so you can redraft parts if necessary.

Here are some 'dos' and 'don'ts':

DO wherever possible, use their language and their descriptive terms. Avoid jargon familiar to you but which may be unfamiliar to them. Don't use acronyms or abbreviations.

DO exactly as they ask. Fill in all the fields (put 'n/a' if not applicable, but don't leave it blank). Ensure you supply every enclosure they request. Check enclosures are signed and dated if necessary (e.g. constitution).

If they ask you to post the application, or submit it by email, but not by fax, don't fax it. If they ask you only to type in the boxes, only type in the boxes...

DON'T either underplay or inflate the budget. A budget that looks unfeasibly small rings as many alarm bells as one that looks too big – they are experts and will reject any unrealistic looking figures.

DON'T assume they know anything about you or your project, or even this kind of project. Explain it clearly.

DON'T rush it. It will save time in the long run.

When you have completed the form in rough, try to read it through objectively. Is it clear? Are the figures accurate? Then show it to someone else who knows nothing about the project and see how well they understand it. Then type up (don't write by hand) the final form, check it again, make a photocopy for your records, write a concise covering letter, again ensure you are enclosing everything they have asked for, including any supporting material, and send it off.

This advice applies to the 'big funders'; the same rules basically apply to smaller bodies. Some of these may not supply a form but will want a letter. They may not supply guidelines. In this case make sure your application letter (which shouldn't be much longer than two pages of A4) is a digest of the information you would supply in a form: what you're doing; who's involved; who benefits and how. Use your 'aims, objectives and methods'. Mention any other sources of funding or support. Enclose your budget, your constitution, accounts (if you have them) or the organisation's most recent bank statement. (Even if the cupboard is bare, a bank statement shows you don't have thousands already, and that you have set up an account and are going about things properly.) Include anything else which might be helpful, such as press clippings, reports of previous events involving the same organizers/leaders. Again, get someone unrelated to the project to read it for you. Double check it for errors and omissions. Make sure it is addressed to an individual, copy and send.

Sources of funding – principal award-makers and their aims

Please check out the relevant websites for guidelines and application forms.

Arts Council Funding

Arts Council England is the national development agency for the arts in England, distributing public money from Government and the National Lottery.

> Our grants are for individuals, arts organisations and other people who use the arts in their work. They support activities that engage people in England or that help artists and arts organisations in England to carry out their work.

www.artscouncil.org.uk

Creative Scotland (a new body, formed by amalgamating Arts Council Scotland and Scottish Screen) will:

- invest in talent • invest in education • invest in places

We are committed to investing in and developing the arts, screen and creative industries in Scotland and playing a lead role in promoting the value and importance of these to everyone.

www.creativescotland.com

Arts Council of Wales is the country's funding and development agency for the arts, investing public funding allocated to them by the Welsh Assembly Government and Lottery funds.

We support and develop high quality arts activity... We are the national voice for the arts in Wales, making sure that people are fully aware of the quality, value and importance of the country's arts. Our job is to ensure that the contribution of the arts is recognised, valued and celebrated.

www.artswales.org.uk

Arts Council of Northern Ireland is the lead development agency for the arts in Northern Ireland.

We are the main support for artists and arts organisations, offering a broad range of funding opportunities through our Exchequer and National Lottery funds.

www.artscouncil-ni.org

Lottery Grants Programmes

Awards for All is a Lottery grants programme aimed at local communities.

Awards for All, England offers grants of between £300 and £10,000 for projects. It is for voluntary and community groups, schools and health organisations, parish and town council:

Our Awards for All programme aims to help improve local communities and the lives of people most in need. To achieve our aim we want to fund projects that meet one or more of the following outcomes:

People have better chances in life – with better access to training and development to improve their life skills.

Stronger communities – with more active citizens working together to tackle their problems.

Improved rural and urban environments – which communities are better able to access and enjoy.

Healthier and more active people and communities.

www.awardsforall.org.uk/england

Awards for All, Scotland

Puts lottery money back into local communities by giving grants of between £500 and £10,000. We fund projects that improve opportunities for people to take part in arts, sport and community activities and can fund a wide range of organisations... We can fund projects that meet one or more of the outcomes for Scotland:

People have better chances in life.

Communities are safer, stronger and more able to work together to tackle inequalities.

People have better and more sustainable services and environments.

People and communities are healthier.

www.awardsforall.org.uk/scotland

Awards for All, Wales aims to:

Support community activity – by helping communities to meet their needs through voluntary action, self-help projects, local facilities or events. (By communities we mean people in a local area or people who

share a common interest or need.)

Extend access and participation – by encouraging more people to become actively involved in local groups and projects, and by supporting activities that aim to be open and accessible to everyone who wishes to take part.

Increase skill and creativity – by supporting activities which help to develop people and organisations, improve skills and raise standards.

Improve the quality of life – by supporting local projects that improve people's opportunities, health, welfare, environment or local facilities, especially those most disadvantaged in society.

www.awardsforall.org.uk/wales

Awards for all, Northern Ireland

The main aim of the programme is to bring real improvements to communities and to the lives of people most in need by funding projects which involve people in their communities, bringing them together to enjoy a wide range of charitable, community, educational, environmental and health-related activities.

www.awardsforall.org.uk/northernireland

Big Lottery Fund – what they say:

We are committed to bringing real improvements to communities and to the lives of people most in need.

www.biglotteryfund.org.uk

Applying to Trust Funds

A full list of grant-making trusts can be found in *The Directory of Grant Making Trusts*, published by the Charities Aid Foundation and revised every year, or *Guide to the Major Trusts*, Volumes 1 and 2 published by the Directory of Social Change – your local library's reference section should have these or other useful sources. (Make sure you are using the most up-to-date edition and then further research the trusts you think look possible candidates on the internet.)

All the same advice about applying to statutory bodies and companies applies. Do your homework: adapt your approach to the particular interests of the trust; study the interests of those that look like possibilities and find out who they have funded in the past and whether you are a likely candidate; ring them up and see whether an informal discussion on the phone would be appropriate before writing. Be aware that trustees may meet far less frequently than other bodies (perhaps only once a year) so you have to get these applications in ASAP. Trusts may have a more emotive core than other bodies (they are often derived from legacies from philanthropists) and often like to feel that the effects of the things they fund (or help to fund) will extend beyond the people immediately involved. You may find yourself making a more personal appeal to very specific aims – if you do think you fit their criteria don't be afraid to show your (or the group's) enthusiasm for the project, the particular energy behind it, and the sense that it is a good thing, for its own sake. Point out that what they want and what you want are the same thing: you can help each other realise your mutual aims.

Sponsorship by individuals or companies

Depending on the size and kind of your production, you may be looking for large sums from one or two businesses, or a number of small sums from many. Let's consider large businesses first. Is there any point applying to a large business for sponsorship if it has no local connection? The answer is probably 'no', *but* if the theme of your play has some connection with their business, you may have a way in. You might get sponsorship from a washing powder manufacturer for a play about a strike in a laundry, for example. Your angle with local businesses is that they are part of the community and you hope they would support (and, importantly, benefit by being seen to support) a community project. You need to make them feel that this is something exciting and worth supporting. You need to look at the project through their eyes when you outline – clearly and simply – your plans. Businesses are used to expecting some kind of commercial benefit from any investment, so you are going to have to 'sell' a non-commercial benefit, which must depend on how they will be perceived by being associated. Offering free advertising in your programme and free tickets to sponsors are also gestures you can make which cost you nothing.

Local businesses need to be approached with an emphasis on them being part of the community which is putting on the play. For example, you could draft your all-purpose opening letter beginning:

> *Ourtown* Community Play is approaching you because *Ourtown* Handling Solutions is well-known as an important/high profile/well-regarded company [or, if an old business – an historically significant part of the local economy] and we feel sure you would like to know of a unique opportunity to support a local initiative.

You could then go on to explain that this is a non-profit-making enterprise, and how it aims to benefit the community – this makes it clear that their money would be going to a good cause, and not just in someone's pocket. If you have got any Unique Selling Points – such as having engaged the co-operation of a well-known name to support or be involved in the project – now is the time to exploit them shamelessly. Establish your group's credibility. If you have already secured co-operation, funding or support from other organisations or businesses, mention this. Businesses, like the rest of us, are attracted by the idea of something new, especially if it is something big and new, but at the same time want to be reassured that there is something tried and tested behind it, so include anything which enhances the project's credibility. (People may like to watch an experiment, but very few people want to fund one.)

Say you expect widespread local media coverage (big plus) and will be mentioning your sponsors in your publicity. Above all, inspire confidence: don't say 'if successful' or in any way suggest the production might not happen (even if you are anxious). Make it seem inevitable and that you are inviting them on board to be part of something exciting. Be courteous and persuasive, and not bullying or arrogant. Don't get carried away with the things that appeal to you about the project – think of what will appeal to them. Don't ask for a – or mention the word – 'donation': this implies giving money away with no return – you want 'sponsorship', because that implies a relationship between what they are doing and what you are doing. Show your draft letter to other people to check there is nothing hectoring or amateurish in its tone.

Now you have got your basic letter, research your targets. If yours is a small community, make a list of everyone who advertises in your local paper and parish magazine; walk down your high street and note all the shops and businesses; don't drive past a sign outside a house that advertises a plasterer, or a plumber, or whatever, without making a note of the details; use the internet to identify local businesses which may be invisible to the naked eye. Business parks, especially in rural areas, are often overlooked, as they tend to be island-like, off main roads and set apart from the town centre, so explore these too. This is your primary small business hit list. Depending on your initial success, you can move on to surrounding, associated, communities if necessary, but what you have done will already have represented a lot of work, and a lot of stamps – don't forget letters cost money, and you haven't got any, yet. (Incidentally, in a small community, sending a letter by post to an address ten minutes' walk from the address it was sent from can suggest you are spending any money you *do* get on the wrong things. Delivering things by hand, where possible, implies you have made an effort, and is cheaper.) Get your team of helpers to identify any of your potential sponsors whom they know – even if they are just regular customers of a particular shop, or the owner of the business is a neighbour. It is harder to say 'no' to someone you know, so have a known 'face' deliver the letter, ideally with a brief verbal explanation of what it's about. However, before you deliver or post your letter, you need to find out who is likely to be in a position to make a decision about sponsorship, as *wherever possible* letters should be addressed to an individual. Personalised letters statistically stand a far greater chance of achieving a positive outcome. This means ringing them up or emailing them (you may be able to get the right contact information from a company website).

All the same rules which apply to drafting a letter apply to an approach by telephone – except that this has to be a lot briefer. If this kind of thing is new to you, it can be a bit nerve-wracking, so here are some tips for making first contact by telephone. Write down your essential message and have it in front of you when you call. When the receptionist answers, if s/he gives her/his name, write it down, and use it when you say goodbye or if you have to call back. Tell the receptionist you are writing to Ourtown Handling Solutions inviting them to become a sponsor of a unique community project – to whom should you address the letter? Is it possible to speak to that person now? If so, again, don't go into masses of detail, and pick up on anything which might connect them to the production. If there has already been something in the local paper or on local radio about it, you can say, 'I don't know whether you heard the piece on Radio Ourtown on Tuesday,' or 'It's quite likely that some of your employees' children might be involved, through the Ourtown school…'

The best approach is to think about what you dislike about cold calling, and avoid it. Don't sound as though you are reading from a script; make sure you are well prepared in case of any questions; be unfailingly pleasant, don't hang up before they do. Though you may be calling *your* twentieth person, it is *their* first call from you. Don't sound as if it's a formula, or say you're 'ringing round' – it's an individual approach. Don't let the phone call end without you having spoken to the relevant person, or having got the name of the person to whom you need to address your letter. Try to maintain an enthusiastic tone – don't make calls when you are tired, unless you know you can pick yourself up. Yours will not be the only call they get on a daily basis asking for something – make your approach sparkle.

With small businesses (which may often be a one-person enterprise) approaching many for a little may be better than approaching a few for a lot (or even a lot for a lot). We made up about a fifth of our budget from sponsorship from small amounts from small businesses in 2009. We offered three tiers of sponsorship: GOLD (£50), FRANKINCENSE (£25) and MYRRH (£10) – sponsors were named and thanked prominently in the programme, and gold sponsors got two free front row tickets for the night of their choice. It involved a great deal of leg work and administrative time on our part, but asking for relatively modest sums from many seemed to pay off and, as this was the first time we failed to secure a Lottery grant (Awards For All had changed their criteria to preclude 'repeat events'), we were very grateful for every penny.

A final word on funding applications

Don't wait to hear from one source of funding before you approach another; you may find yourself running out of time. If you make a successful application, always write immediately to thank them and let them know how

you got on when the event is over. (Some will ask you to give specific feedback and may provide a separate form for this.) File both 'no' and 'yes' responses – this prevents duplicate approaches and may be useful in the future.

Other organisations and individuals and raising money yourself

Other community organisations may be willing to offer support but are often likely to be as strapped for cash as you are. However, you can elicit their support in other ways. You may be able to borrow staging blocks from a school; lights from a village hall; expertise from a rotary club; costumes or props from a local theatre company... think creatively – who has got what you want? How can you persuade them to lend or give it to you?

There may be individuals who can help you, either by sponsoring the production with cash, or with their name and personal endorsement. These will be individual to each place, so depend on your wits and local knowledge. Finally, you can put on fundraising events yourself. To suggest these here would take another chapter, so consult your support base, make the figure you need to raise known, and get them thinking and working. You personally (the fundraiser) are likely to be too busy to get deeply involved with fundraising events per se, so delegate.

Just as wood is the fuel that warms you twice (once when you chop it, again when you burn it), consider events with double payback. For the last two years we have organized a 'singing day', where people (a large proportion of whom usually don't sing) come together for one day in which they become a choir, and then perform to an audience in the evening. Participants in the choir-for-a-day pay a modest fee for a day's singing and the attendant amusement and entertainment, and the audience pay a modest charge for tickets to come and hear them in the evening. We invite other local choirs to support us at the concert, include an element of community singing, where we all become a giant choir, and run a bar (always a solid earner, as well as a loosener of inhibitions about communal singing) and, again, this raises about a fifth of our budget. Everybody wins, and not only financially: a proportion of the choir-for-a-day will volunteer for the community play choir (now knowing there is no mystery or fear in it); the singers have had a great day and enjoyed the applause and approbation of the audience; the audience have had an enjoyable evening; and, importantly, the wider community is aware of our efforts to raise money on our own behalf. Arranging an activity like this is also a good thing to be able to report to potential funders: it shows not only that you are raising funds yourself, but that you are putting into practise the same values you are looking for them to support in your application for funds. Table-top sales and other more humble activities are not to be dismissed: we do these and the fact that your community play has a profile at any event is a plus. Raising awareness of your existence and your dedication to 'making it happen' are actually of incalculable value, if all you take home is £30. And it's still £30.

Non-artistic benefits of community theatre

Though they are generally recognised by those involved, no research has been done on the social benefits of the community play, but it is clear that they are both wide-ranging and profound. In this section I am taking artistic achievements as read and focusing on these benefits, by drawing together evidence of the effects of theatrical and musical participation for different social groups who might be expected to participate. Though of interest for its own sake, the purpose of this section is to provide you with material you may find useful in demonstrating the social benefits of your project to potential funders of which they may be unaware. I will begin at the beginning, with children.

Jonas Basom, an American educator, actor and director, has studied a wide range of research on the (often largely unappreciated) benefits of drama as part of the school curriculum and finds widespread evidence that it has the following measurable effects: developing confidence and trust, creative thinking and interpretation of material, discussion and negotiation skills, quick thinking and memory; promoting compassion and tolerance, skills of sustained concentration, perseverance and self-control; enhancing expression, articulation and other communication skills as well as co-ordination and both physical and mental flexibility and agility; reducing stress and releasing tension and aggression in a safe environment. These benefits can easily be

extrapolated to apply to children engaging with drama outside school and to adults as well. In other words, here is some evidence that participation in theatre is, apart from anything else, literally good for you, having a positive impact on psychological, emotional, social and cognitive development in a wide range of ways.

Participation in theatre clearly results in valuable and recognised social functions that are not confined to aesthetic or artistic benefits. Anecdotal evidence also tells us that children who specialise in drama tend to present themselves much more confidently than their peers at (non-drama related) university and job interviews, in class presentations and when required to do public speaking, while common sense and experience inform us that there are children who struggle with academic subjects and the one place they can shine is on stage (as others may on the field or pitch or cricket ground). Theatre Studies (or Drama, in old money) offers children in many respects a parallel experience to what the community play offers adults. It is demanding, challenging, confidence building, harmony promoting, etc. and develops many skills transferable to other areas of life. The most common response from participants, post project, is that they have done something they had never thought themselves capable of, learnt a great deal about themselves and others, and that it has given them a new and more positive view of their community. Hours of therapy might achieve the same results, at vastly greater expense, and not prove nearly as much fun.

To leap from children to the other end of the spectrum, the myriad benefits of participation in theatre specifically for senior citizens are finally beginning to be appreciated. These too can be easily referred to the benefits of the open door community play. Bonnie Vorenberg, an expert in gerontology and theatre, has studied the recent phenomenon of the growth in theatre groups specifically for older people in the U.S.A. and has found clear evidence that participants gain mentally, physically and socially. Quite apart from the exercise involved, for both body and mind, theatre participation offers opportunities for social interaction in an age group where, for example, a poor or limited social network increases the risk of dementia by 60%. Vorenberg states confidently that participation in community theatre is 'better than a trip to the doctor' for many older people – and gives them a sense of perspective about

their own ailments which far less frequently form the principal topic of conversation. 'Seniors' also often report that their theatre involvement helped them get off anti-depressants or blood pressure medications.

If we can recognise the values of participating in drama for the older and younger members of our society, we could project (if we didn't already know) that there are related benefits for the rest of us.

The value of play (as opposed to 'the play')

I would argue for the value of 'play' itself. We know that small children learn about and negotiate their role in the world through play; as adults we have learnt to see 'play' as childish, and dignify it by refiguring the activities we choose to do that are not work, and which we enjoy purely for their own sake and the pleasure of doing them, as 'hobbies' or 'interests'. Even bar room banter, which can extract an evening's entertainment out of one of the regulars having had a haircut, is a form of play – but it's called 'stick' (in a

British pub, anyway); nevertheless it's a game of wit for its own sake which can last all night.

In fact, involvement in an actual, theatrical play is the closest many people will come to re-engaging with play in its real sense. Getting involved with a play gives ordinary adults (by which I mean people who are not professional actors) the license (because it is a structured activity with an end result which benefits others) to engage in a game of make believe, and the attendant endless potential for creativity, both personal and collective. They get to pretend, to dress up, to sing and dance, possibly, to show off, but primarily, to pretend. This alone, I maintain, has incalculable value.

I recently (at forty-seven years old) took the role of a fairy in an open-air non-professional production of *A Midsummer Night's Dream*. The director had recruited his entire fairy band from middle-aged village women, necessarily of various shapes and sizes and perhaps not as nimble at 'flitting' as fairies might be expected to be. There was, of course, method in his madness; we were not pretty fairies but were rather woodland spirits, who perhaps had seen more of mortal ways and were wiser to them than more juvenile sprites might have been (well, you've got to work with what you've got, but he made it work).

Having not performed (except in the choir and the crowd in our community play) for several years I was astonished at how exciting and thrilling and rewarding I found the experience. The fairies – who quickly became a gang of fairies – 'played' not only in front of the audience, but backstage of course, as this interplay and badinage between cast members is all part and parcel of the company experience. And that is another of the benefits – being part of a company of players, and being licensed to 'play' – that cannot be quantified.

Before leaving this subject, it is worth saying that we may be uniquely positioned as a society to benefit from everything the community play has to offer, and may actually need it now more than ever. It's widely observed that the social networks our grandparents took for granted have declined: our extended families are often not easily accessible, we may have less face-to-face contact with co-workers, we may well know characters in a TV soap opera better than we know our neighbours. When our time becomes pressured

(and we are told we are the most cash rich/time poor generation ever) the short-cuts we take further contract our social opportunities: we drive, rather than walk, evacuating the possibility of an encounter with another walker; we can 'self-serve' in silence at the supermarket, or even shop without leaving home at all; we can 'text' rather than speak, and increasingly our dealings with the world preclude conversations with real people, and once verbal (if remote) interactions are reduced to pressing buttons on the telephone keypad at one end and a range of recorded messages at the other. We have more choices before us than ever before, but though it is easier and easier to get what we want materially, it is harder and harder to get hold of 'a real person'. And because we can bring the world to our door, it is decreasingly incumbent on us to step outside it, and we too become less accessible, and in effect absent as social beings.

So how do we regain our 'social capital'? One way, certainly, is through re-engaging with our community through the community play.

Valuing Community Theatre

I emphasise all these potential social benefits of theatre because they are not widely appreciated by those we need to persuade. The difficulty is this: while bodies that fund the Arts may be peopled by those who are most likely to be aware of these factors, they are primarily funding *arts* projects (and are consequently looking to fund professionals with quantifiable and deliverable outcomes, based on the body of work that artist has already produced, or their perceived potential) rather than community projects. Conversely, those bodies that fund *community* projects may well be only dimly aware of these social aspects of theatre. They may think that a community play might be a 'good thing' because a community pulls together towards a common goal, but they may have no concept of the myriad other benefits to the individual and the community. It will only be as a result of many of us relentlessly insisting on the reality and importance of these benefits that this will change.

A very similar case (and one underpinned by scientific research) can be made for the widely unappreciated social value of singing. Singing is the most democratic and accessible musical form, as it depends on the voice, an instrument everyone already owns and can play. A society which values music should be promoting the myriad benefits of choral singing in every village, town and city – it's cheap, it's easy and there's no excuse not to. The success of television programmes like *Last Choir Standing* and the extraordinary Gareth Malone's *The Choir* testify to the appetite for choral singing and the clear practical possibility of making it a reality in *any* community. It is said that there are currently more choirs in Britain than there are fish-and-chip

shops, but only a tiny proportion get any kind of public funding, and membership fees can be steep. Instead, funding for music is focused largely on professional projects, again relegating the community to the role of spectator/listener and implying that for music-making to be valued, it has to be performed by professionals.

There are, however, many reasons to value singing. The benefits for children of singing were assumed rather than promoted and attracted little attention in the days when people of my generation and older routinely sang together daily in school assembly as well as in dedicated music lessons. The decline of collective worship in schools and the demands of the National Curriculum subsequently progressively squeezed singing to the margins (if not out) of the curriculum in many schools. Still today, most primary schools do not employ a music specialist and some primary schools have not one member of staff even able to play a simple accompaniment on the piano. The picture has, however, begun to be transformed by the excellent government sponsored 'Sing Up' campaign, which has provided materials and support to enable any primary school teacher to get children singing in schools again.

The effects of the project have been carefully monitored in a study led by Professor Graham Welch (Chair of Music Education at the Institute of Education, University of London) in a two year study. He found that as well as the benefits which might be expected (improved musical competence, more positive attitudes to singing) as the children became better singers they tended to have a much more positive view of themselves, not only as singers, but in general, and developed a stronger sense of social inclusion. An unrelated study in America found that children in choirs had more advanced social skills than those who had never participated. The vast majority of parents said their child's ability to manage his/her emotions and/or read the emotions of others improved after they became choral singers. It would appear that it is not singing alone, but singing collectively, which has significant social benefits for children.

A range of academic literature has addressed the connections between singing and well-being in adults, finding that regular singing can enhance mood, happiness and emotional well-being, and reduce stress and depression. In two separate surveys of choral singers, the majority believed that singing had contributed to their 'personal' or 'mental' well-being, while common responses in a third included variations of statements such as: singing 'helps make me a happier person', 'gives a positive attitude to life' and 'lifts mood and helps to forget problems'.

The idea that singing can cheer you up is of course not a new one: think of slaves in cotton-fields, convicts on chain-gangs, soldiers in trenches, civilians in air raid shelters: singing is a collective response to a communal situation and can lift the spirits and alleviate sorrow. It's no accident that the taunting musical chant from football terraces 'You're Not Singing Anymore!' refers to the loss of morale by fans on the losing side. So we know singing makes us feel better as individuals, and bonds us together as a community. Integrating singing in the community play accesses these benefits for the whole cast and promotes cohesion, a sense of shared endeavour and confidence. A community choir may even grow out of your play.

However, there are other, scientifically proven, benefits, as increasingly medical research shows that singing has measurable positive impacts on health and is quite literally 'good for you':

- Singing provides a 'workout', it's an aerobic activity that increases oxygenation in the blood stream and exercises major muscle groups in the upper body (including the lungs and heart), even when sitting. A Harvard and Yale study showed that choral singing increased the life expectancy of the population of New Haven, Connecticut. (The report concluded that this was because singing promoted both a healthy heart and an enhanced mental state.)

- Singing reduces stress levels through the action of the endocrine system which is linked to our sense of emotional well-being. Singing causes the body to produce endorphins (the much vaunted 'feel good' hormones), having a similar effect to brisk exercise (or eating chocolate, but without the calories, of course).

- Singing can increase lung capacity, clears respiratory tubes.

- Singing can increase mental alertness through greater oxygenation.

- Perhaps most astonishingly, one study at the University of California has reported higher levels of immune system proteins in the saliva of choristers (after performing a complex Beethoven masterwork) while another in Germany showed the same effect from blood samples taken before and after singing a Bach oratorio.

I mention these benefits in such detail and at such length not because I wish to 'murder to dissect' and suck all the magic out of the musical/theatrical experience by analysing its measurable social benefits, but because you may increasingly find yourself having to emphasise the contribution to physical and mental well-being your production will make as health becomes more of an issue with funders. You may sense or 'know' that the community play brings many benefits on many levels, but you may well have to spell these out, for the benefit of those who need to be able to tick particular boxes.

●

3. Core Team, Venue and Dates

You have already (hopefully) recruited an individual or a team who will take care of the financial aspects of the production, fulfilling the role of fundraiser and being in charge of the budget. You will also need someone (a good communicator, with a creative as well as a commercial eye) to be in charge of publicity. Now you need a writer, a director and a producer, not necessarily in that order.

The role of the director is to:
- be the 'artistic director', handling all the creative decisions
- take 'acting' rehearsals
- manage, prepare and support the performers
- work closely with the writer and producer

The role of the producer is to:
- have overall control of the practical aspects of the production
- co-ordinate its constituent elements
- handle administrative aspects
- be responsible for communications

If you are able to run to it, a director's assistant and a production assistant (or two) are very desirable.

A director's assistant should basically assist the director in any way the director finds useful, and different directors have different needs. One director may want the assistant to 'sit on the script' in rehearsals, so that the director can observe the actors without having to follow the script, and can refer to the assistant for the clarification of a line or a cue, for example. A second director may want the assistant to take all notes that come up in rehearsal. A third may just want frequent cups of tea and someone to discuss things with. A fourth might want something more like an assistant director – someone they can delegate bits of direction to: managing a crowd scene, perhaps, or working with an actor or small group of actors on a particular piece of business.

A production assistant assists the producer in all the practical, administrative and logistical roles listed above. The production assistant is the ideal person to have a complete and up-to-date contact record for everyone involved in the production – name, address, e-mail address, telephone number (home, work and mobile) – so that they can be immediately contacted in case of a change to the schedule, or any problem. If it is not them, someone who will be at every rehearsal (the producer or director's assistant) must have this with them at all times.

The writer will of course have responsibility for producing a script. This will need scheduling so that an agreed version (between director, producer and writer) of the script is ready before the start of rehearsals. Especially if you are paying the writer, it is important that the arrangement between the writer and the CPA is clear. The CPA needs to set out in writing exactly what it is asking for – and what it is offering. The writer needs to know things like the approximate running time of the show, the types and size of cast (if you are including children, the writer needs to know this), any staging limitations or possibilities which are outside ordinary expectations, etc. Are you paying the writer expenses on top of any fee? If so, there needs to be a cap on these. The CPA needs to state deadlines; depending on how far advanced the details of the idea are, you might need deadlines for some or all of the following:

- an outline of the play (plot and characters)
- a scene-by-scene summary
- a first draft

- a second draft
- a 'final' draft.

What the subject of the play will be will very likely have been decided already, but will the CPA offer research to the writer or expect the writer to do this him/herself? Will the CPA offer the opportunity to 'workshop' scenes as they are developing? Who exactly is going to make decisions about the script? (No writer should be exposed to a committee, and whoever is passing comment on the script needs to be competent to do so. All script notes – whoever they come from – should be channelled through one person to the writer (the producer or director, ideally, depending on temperament and the quality of relationships which already exist). Multiple critics will lead to contradictory notes, which are both demoralising and useless to the writer. Again, if you are paying your writer and have a formal contract, it is advisable to establish a potential cut-off point early on in the process, at which date if differences between the writer and the CPA are too great, all deals are off. (There is advice on writing the script and the process of consultation and redrafting in the next chapter.)

All these things also have to be considered if you are employing/recruiting a composer. Where money is going to change hands, the brief/contract needs to be as watertight as possible. It doesn't have to be daunting, or full of legalese – make it clear and simple, stating a clear chain of decision-making, and be unambiguous about dates and deadlines. If things are going well you can afford, in the event, to be flexible about these; if things are going badly, you may need them. Just make sure that as well as planning for the best outcome, you have a back-up plan and a get-out clause if relations with your writer (or composer) deteriorate irretrievably. A strong script is the rock on which you will build your play, and a good working relationship with the writer is vital.

If you have a designer (who will design the 'look' of the production and the set) this needs to be someone who can work closely with director, producer and costume personnel. If you don't have a designer, the look of the production is going to depend on the director and the costume designer, who may also be the wardrobe mistress or master. Costume/wardrobe need to be brought on board at an early stage too, so that there is time to achieve the desired overall visual effects. Director, designer and costume/wardrobe need to be singing from the same hymn sheet from the very beginning.

Other creative roles, such as band leader, choir leader, choreographer – if applicable – need to take responsibility for their area of expertise, working with the producer on practical issues (e.g. when and where they can rehearse) and the director on artistic ones.

The producer should, with the co-operation of the core team, draw up a schedule of what should be ready by when and check that these are done on target. The director and wardrobe, for example, need dates for: discussing costumes; making decisions about costumes; looking together at 'finished' costumes and agreeing changes where necessary; reviewing the final costumes. Similarly, targets are necessary for the designer and director to discuss developments on the set. Directors can be both busy and elusive when not taking rehearsals and it is the producer's job to make sure there are fixed dates when they will observe the choir, the band, the dancers, etc. in their own rehearsals before these groups join the full rehearsals. It is also important to facilitate opportunities for those in charge of music, dancing, children, etc. to see what is happening in the main rehearsals, so they get a sense of the overall feel of the production and the intention of the director, so their contributions will complement it and – importantly – so they don't start to feel left out of the loop.

All this consultation is necessary not only to reduce the workload involved in remedying things which have gone (unsupervised or unmediated) off in the wrong direction, but to reduce the inevitable cost of putting things right. Money and time are your most precious resources; scheduling regular consultations (and ensuring they happen) between different arms or departments of the production prevents both being wasted.

Other important team members will be your lighting and sound designer and operator and your stage manager. Ideally, all of these should have assistants, but these need not be experts; a lighting operator may merely need a spare pair of hands to work a follow-spot, for example. (A more detailed account of the roles of lighting and sound designers and operators is given in Chapter 6.)

The role of the stage manager varies in different productions, according to how 'hands-on' the producer is, but is generally in charge of the set and the props, organising scene changes and much of the practical work backstage. S/he requires a strong sense of initiative and may well be responsible for tasks as varied as calling or cueing actors for entrances and organising rehearsals. In a community play, the stage manager may find themselves picking up the slack no-one else has thought of (ours doubles as the set designer). Needless to say, a good stage manager is worth their weight in gold.

Choosing a venue

Some points to consider if you are not using a purpose-built theatre:

- If yours is a local story, is there a location which might be strongly symbolic?

- Is there a building which has architectural features which would enhance the production?

- Is there a venue you could get to use free of charge or for a modest fee?

- Is it going to be possible to hang lights and install sound equipment? (There may be practical difficulties or restrictions in the hiring agreement, especially if the building is listed.)

- Are you going to have difficulty getting a licence to perform in the venue?

- Will you be able to fit everyone in? You need to be aware that buildings will often have maximum numbers imposed by fire regulations, and limits will be imposed on outside areas by local authorities or the police for health and safety reasons. Don't forget that your cast needs to be included in the number of people attending. Also be aware that event insurers will limit audience numbers, if they consider the venue at all hazardous. (An open air promenade production in large private gardens might, for example, be restricted to only fifty spectators per performance, which, unless you are doing a huge number of performances, will be unfeasible.)

- If you are going to need to erect temporary structures (e.g. a beer tent; portable toilets) is there space for them?

- Have you got necessary backstage facilities?

- Is there sufficient parking?

- Is there disabled access?

- Are you likely to have problems with noise (neighbours disturbing you, or you disturbing neighbours)?

- Check that the venue is not only available for your performance dates, but that you will have time in it to build the set and install lighting and sound (and take it all out again), as well as hold your later rehearsals in the venue.

Don't be daunted – perfect performance spaces are few and far between. And have the cheek to ask for a venue for nothing, if you have a low budget – after all, it is a *community* play. We manage a cast of around 100 and 200 audience members with only one lavatory in the building (having no interval, though, and no bar helps); there is only a small vestry which could be described as 'backstage'; parking is ad hoc. You really have to work out

whether you can manage with what is there and improvise as necessary. Then book it for the dates you need as early as possible.

It is also worth considering whether your venue is going to be comfortable for the audience. If your audience (let alone your cast) is cold, you have an uphill struggle on your hands. (Having said that, during the outdoor production of *A Midsummer Night's Dream* mentioned earlier, the audience was at its most appreciative, and the cast at its most valiant, on the night it rained relentlessly – if things get really bad, a kind of Blitz spirit can kick in.) If (as has been our experience) your venue is generally cold and uncomfortable, be prepared to go the extra mile to make it as warm and comfortable as possible for the audience. (Until recently, our church was so cold in the winter that costumes could not be left overnight, as they were too damp to wear the following night; and you could see your breath at rehearsals. There was heating, but it was extremely expensive to run it, so we saved our electricity budget for rehearsals involving children, the final rehearsals and performances only, and then brought in extra heaters. We also put the kneelers on the pews to make the seating less uncomfortable.) Barns, warehouses, churches and the open air can all be cold environments: warning the audience in advance to wrap up well is always wise.

When preparing the venue for the performances (if it is not usually used in this way) you may need to move things about – these will need to be put back where they came from when the play is over. It is a good idea to take pictures of what goes where, unless you have an excellent memory or can take good notes. If you are using a venue free of charge the very least you can do is leave it as you found it. You may also need to put up signs (showing the way to the toilets, for example, or asking people to turn off their mobile phones). You need to think about where your box office will go, and try to arrange it so that the audience is not queuing outside. Are you numbering seats and tickets? Have you got areas where people in wheelchairs will have good sight-lines? (Health and safety considerations will be addressed further on.)

Dates for the production

Try to avoid clashes with events likely to involve your performers or spectators. If participation of a school is envisioned, they have very busy calendars, and will need to be consulted well in advance, as will any other participating organisation (e.g. choirs). You need to allow time to:

- produce a script.

- put together your production team.

- raise funds (getting all the information needed for funding applications takes time, and once the application is submitted it may take several weeks and possibly months before you get a decision).

- publicise your project (in the first phase, to attract participants; in the second phase to attract audiences).

- hold casting sessions and then rehearsals.

- obtain permissions, licenses and complete other administrative jobs.

Be realistic about how long all this will take, but also be aware that many of these things can be happening simultaneously. Draw up a preliminary timetable of what needs to be done when; the script, recruitment publicity and fundraising are among the things your team needs to start tackling first.

You also need to decide how many performances the play is going to run for. It may be financially more viable to run it for more rather than fewer nights. For example, if you are hiring lighting equipment for, say, two weeks (allowing for set-up, final rehearsals, performances and get-out), three performances may cost no more in terms of lighting hire, than one, but may raise three times as much in ticket sales.

Once you have a team, a venue and dates, your project becomes inevitable. Now you need the right script...

●

4. Writing the Script

Choosing a subject

The chances are that you are reading this book because you have already thought of something you want to do a play about – perhaps you have chosen a subject, or have a script already. If not, favourite and successful subjects for community plays are, as we have seen, episodes in local history. A local subject uniquely engages both participants and audience. Local historians and historical societies are mines of information; both the library service and local newspaper archives are also rich sources.

I dipped into one aspect of local history when I read the old log books of our village school (for an unrelated project) and discovered that you don't even need to be looking for a fully developed 'story'. Starting points for a plot or a character for a play could be suggested from just one sentence. In September 1890 the Headteacher wrote: 'Admitted seven children, four of whom are boys from Dr Barnardo's Home.' Further research into the school registers showed that over a thirty year period Dr Barnardo had sent 110 children to live with families in the village, which made them a significant proportion of the population. There was the basis of a story: abandoned children from urban slums deposited in an isolated rural community, which was almost certainly unprepared for what traumas these children might have endured. In July 1899, Alice Jackson failed to come to school because she had 'no boots to come in'. There was a character. Was Alice any better off than the Barnardo's boys? And so on. With the various details of outbreaks of epidemic diseases, disputes between staff and school board, a romance between two teachers which resulted in joint dismissal, truculent parents, a strike over school closure, there was material in those old books for several plays. Once you start looking, you will be fighting off subjects (and their champions).

At the other end of the scale, a play with a so-called universal theme can also be appropriate. (Why not Shakespeare?) The medieval Mystery plays are classic examples of this, although the popularity of their revivals in modern times has been strongest in the places where they were originally performed, so they now benefit from both a widely accessible narrative and a local historical association. Both Chester and York revived their Mystery plays after centuries of neglect in 1951 as part of the Festival of Britain celebrations, since when Chester has performed them every five years and York annually. Lichfield performs a play every three years using fragments of the town's own medieval plays and borrowings from more complete cycles. The 'N-Town' play cycle is performed regularly in Lincoln and Wakefield has revived its cycle occasionally, while Durham recently recreated ten of the plays for a modern audience.

It may even be that there are old plays still in existence associated with your region which might provide a starting point. Whatever you choose will give you a reason for doing a play on this subject, in this place, at this time. The only other criterion is that it requires a lot of people to be in it, who are not regular performers. A cast of five is not a community play. A play put on by an amateur dramatics society is not a community play. The nearest thing to a naturally arising community play is probably a village or otherwise local non-professional pantomime, and that is not a community play because although it may be open to all newcomers as performers, its social role is generally more important than its artistic aspirations. The true community play, for it to have value as a play, aims for a professional standard of production from non-professional participants.

Some community plays develop their scripts by workshopping situations based on the historical record, and allowing characters to develop through improvisation. First-time performers will find this very challenging and I wouldn't recommend it for stage virgins. Children, however, being much less inhibited, and having an affinity with 'make believe', respond well and in my own script I make room for children to have an input in what their characters say, as it encourages them to think about the situation their characters are in, and act appropriately.

Considering options: including children and music

There are many positive reasons to include children in your production, even if none of the principal characters is a child. Looking at it from a creative angle, children add both interest and realism to any crowd scene. If you are including singing, children's voices add another unique dimension and their participation generally brings a different and refreshing energy. Whether or not your production is going to embrace the participation of children is a vital decision which needs to be made at the earliest stage. You can then incorporate them in the script, rather than make their involvement appear as an afterthought.

Approaching it from a community-value angle, the experience of participating in a community play is likely to be an unforgettable one for a child, and in some small way may compensate for the fact that since the introduction of the National Curriculum, space in the school timetable for music and drama has severely contracted. The participation of children brings many other benefits, including a salutary effect on your adult actors, broadening the potential audience base, drawing parents into the production – aspects which will be discussed further on.

Integrating music in the show is also something to consider now. Whether music is used incidentally, or whether your play becomes a full-blown musical, music – and especially singing – adds a whole new dimension to the production. You may be able to recruit a choir, or build one from scratch – either are ways of involving people who may like to be part of the play without wishing to 'act'. (In our case, we built our own scratch choir for the first three productions and for the last two augmented this with an existing local women's choir.) If you don't have the resources to form a choir or chorus for the production, you can integrate solo songs in the play, and round off with a number sung by the entire cast. There are numerous permutations and ways of getting music into the story.

Instrumentalists can be used to stunningly good effect, and not only to accompany singing. I saw a school production of a musical where – to universal surprise and delight – the town brass band appeared for just one number. Early planning between you, the director and producer, may make it possible to engage local musical groups to make a cameo type appearance – a strategy which is both effective and to which they may be more willing to agree than committing to the weekly rehearsals that full-time involvement in the production would necessarily require.

It's also worth finding out what your cast can do. Among our Roman soldiers we discovered we had a brass player and a drummer. Herod's entrances were made infinitely more dramatic by a uniformed herald and a regimental drummer leading marching soldiers through the audience made the effect much more unsettling.

If you only use musicians to accompany singing, think further than a pianist. You may be able to recruit or form a band for the purpose. While it would be fantastic to involve a pre-existing local orchestra or large choir, they usually have their programmes planned years in advance, and unless you have a very long lead-in to your production it may be impossible to secure them – but don't let that stop you asking. In any case, creating a band or a choir/chorus specifically for the play is all part of the provisional and adventurous nature of the community play: it can be done.

Taking liberties

If you are writing about real historical events you will have to decide the extent to which you are going to stick resolutely to the facts and how much license you have to invent. If it is a well-known story you will attract a lot of criticism by making changes which alter the essential facts, but a slavish adherence to the absolute truth is unlikely to be exciting. The historical record has gaps – often where the ordinary people should be – and your play should bring the story to life by filling in these gaps, building on what is known, and speculating on how people might have responded. Stick to the facts when they are essential, but don't let them get in the way when they aren't.

In our play we have a scene with King Herod and John the Baptist followed a couple of scenes later by one set twenty years earlier, when the Magi visit Herod with news of the star and the prophesied messiah. In the historical record, these were two different Herods, but we have conflated them into one. To make a point of differentiating the two Herods might have satisfied the historical record, but would have very much got in the way of the play, so seemed a justifiable liberty. Depending on how old your story is, there may be aspects of the story that are grounded more in legend than in fact and again you will have to make decisions about what sources you are going to use, or how you are going to manage cherry picking from a range of sources.

As well as building up characters from a very limited amount of information, you may need to invent completely new characters to 'stand for' real historical people. For example, if your play were about a mutiny in which there were seven leaders, all of whom broadly fulfilled the same function, you might choose to concentrate on making three of them fully rounded characters who reflected the broad divisions of opinion within the group. This makes the story more manageable for the audience and also enables you to demonstrate the competing points of view more efficiently. Anything that is likely to confuse the audience needs either to be explained very clearly while avoiding tedium, or, if possible, left out altogether. The most important thing is to avoid sag, and this can happen when you get bogged down in detail. Every scene in the play should fulfil one of two functions: inform character or advance action. A scene that does both is even better. So a scene in which something happens which moves the story forward, but in which we also understand more about the characters, is doing its job. (This rule also applies to songs – they need to be doing a job in the story. Avoid any sense that everything stops while a song 'happens': it can be setting the scene, conveying information/advancing the plot, offering insight into a character, but it can't just be a song for the sake of a song.)

Because our retelling of the Nativity involved jumps backwards and forwards in time, and changes of location without a change of scenery, we

decided early on that we needed a Storyteller figure to lead the audience through the story. There was an added complication in that our play was going to include medieval legends and apocryphal accounts of the story, as well as the well-known narrative. In order to differentiate between these, we gave the Storyteller the role of relating the story as it appears in the Gospels. He opens the play with a direct address to the audience, and links scenes until we get to the point where Joseph is chosen to be Mary's husband, an event which is embellished by the legends. Here the Storyteller finds himself interrupted by women ('gossips', in the medieval sense of female friends/neighbours) who insist on revising the tale as they know it, from the legends. Thereafter the Storyteller is allowed to be largely in charge of the narrative, but defers to the gossips on the colourful detail.

Making the script fit the cast

In our case, we had a very good idea of our story before work began on the script: both the Nativity narrative and its characters are of course widely known, to the extent that we were able to cast three of the parts before the play was even written. The very first approaches we made were to the three ministers of our local churches. (It should be mentioned here, in case you were wondering, that we wanted participants of all and no faith, and that is what we got: a far greater proportion of the cast were not regular church-goers than were, and many were and are atheists and agnostics. The demography of the cast seems to reflect that of the audience and the community as a whole.) At the outset of the project, we envisaged casting the three ministers of the village churches as the three wise men (hereafter 'Magi', as one was a woman). This, we felt, was richly symbolic and would draw in all three churches on an equal footing; it also gave the project some local credibility.

Our dealings with the Magi offer an illustration of how logistical problems can affect the script. It quickly became apparent that there were only three evenings between the beginning of September and the middle of December when all three ministers would be available for rehearsal at the same time. We accommodated this by squeezing in a couple of daytime sessions, but then we didn't have the other characters in the scene, who were at work.

Knowing about their hectic schedules before the play was written meant that I had time to revise my idea of using them in another plotline which would have involved them throughout the play. As it was, we were able to confine their involvement to two key scenes: the visit to Herod, a dialogue-heavy scene, and the Adoration, which was a scene where they had no lines. The lesson from all this is that if you have individuals in mind whose participation is vital to your vision, make sure you have a very clear idea of the limits of their availability (and have secured the highest level of commitment) before you write the script.

A draft of the play for casting purposes need not be complete and should allow room for manoeuvre, not only to accommodate your cast but because changes which occur as a result of the casting session often improve the script. At the casting session when we were looking for two women to play the 'gossips', three women seemed perfectly suitable; moreover they knew each other well and had a good rapport, so we expanded the roles to make parts for three women. In every way three turned out to work better than two, and inadvertently added to the symmetry of the piece: three Magi, three shepherds, three gossips.

The writer should be present not only at casting but at all early rehearsals (ideally, at *all* rehearsals) so that the director can consult about queries and problems on the spot.

Rewriting drafts

Sometimes directors will ask for changes following the first read-through. Others prefer to run a workshop where key scenes can be developed with the help of the performers. A degree of flexibility is required from the writer who has the difficult job of trying to meet the needs of both the artistic team and the performers while keeping his/her original vision of the play in mind. Rewriting the script is always a process of collaboration and some of the strongest ideas emerge from this process.

Casting can throw up a number of issues. For example, our first Mary was an excellent actress but wasn't a singer, and she had an important solo quite early in the play. We therefore created Mary's Friend, who could sing it for her. However, to reduce the rather unsettling effect of suddenly

having a new character pop up just for one song, we used Mary's Friend as a character with whom Mary could interact, so she could voice her anxieties about the arranged marriage with Joseph. During one rehearsal the director noticed the girl playing Mary's Friend in the kitchen, helping the girl playing Mary learn the lines she had with Joseph, when she tells him about the mysterious pregnancy. Hearing Mary's Friend suggesting how Mary should say one of the lines, he had the idea of putting this in the script: that Mary would try out various ways of delivering this awkward news to Joseph by practising with her Friend.

This was easy enough to do, and made Mary's Friend seem less of a device to solve a problem, and the relationship between the two women seems more authentic, as well as doing the practical job of delivering the necessary information. So, if you find you need to create a character to solve a practical problem, make sure they are not stuck out on a limb (for example, with just one song to sing) but find creative ways of integrating them more fully into the story. Mary's Friend worked so well that even when we have had Marys who *can* sing, we have retained the character of Mary's Friend.

Mary and Mary's Friend worked successfully for the first four productions, but in the fifth we were faced with a problem which again arose from the casting session. We had two very good candidates for Mary – one quite feisty and confident girl (more like our first Mary), the other looked right and had a kind of innocence about her (more like our subsequent Marys). Both read well and we were in agonies of indecision, aware that for either of them Mary's Friend would represent a very disappointing alternative, while not making full use of their talents. We therefore decided to work up the part of Mary's Friend into a much more substantial role. In middle-eastern Nativity legends there is a woman with Mary, possibly a midwife, who accompanies the holy family on the flight into Egypt, and Western medieval legends also make much of a midwife as part of the story. So, while we already had a midwife in our story, we felt it was not inauthentic to have Rachel (she now got a name) accompanying Mary. This worked very well, and we got great value from both actresses.

The lesson I took away from this was to remember that first and foremost you want to get the best out of the cast. The script has to serve that end. So, although you can't chop the script about indiscriminately, the writer has to be willing to improvise and adapt his or her material to exploit the available talent. Moreover, as the next example shows, you often don't need to rewrite a lot of the play to achieve this: often one key scene will do the trick.

Here I must briefly digress for a key note to both the writer and director about rehearsals. It is vital that the writer and director have a shared vision of the play and if there are disagreements the cast must be kept blissfully unaware of them. The director must show the writer the respect of not making substantial changes to the script without consulting the writer. The writer must allow the director to make his or her contribution and not defend every word of the script to the death. Both should listen to actors' worries or ideas about the script but resist conspiracies. A united front at all times is vital in inspiring confidence in your cast. Finally, avoid big script changes late in rehearsals if possible. Where, due to unforeseen circumstances, this is necessary, the director should explain the reason for the change to the cast and make sure everyone understands it.

Our last production provided an excellent example of the usefulness of having the writer at rehearsals. When writing the original script we had needed

someone for Herod to interact with and invented Marcus, a senior Roman soldier, to be his right-hand man. (Marcus also provided a link with Rome, as Herod is a regional governor, and a local man.) In the first four productions Marcus hadn't changed much – he was in uniform and generally had a brusquely efficient military style about him. Herod consulted Marcus on courses of action, but appeared to make his own decisions. Herod was cold rather than cruel: a politician, and always with his ear to the ground for signs of discontent.

The short scene in which Herod ordered the massacre of the innocents had always worked well. Marcus tells Herod that the insurgent they've been sent to eliminate turns out to be a baby: does this change the orders? Herod tells him simply to kill all the babies in Bethlehem.. 'Kill *all* the babies, sir?' Marcus queries; 'No,' Herod says, adding, after a moment, 'Just the boys.'

However, the scene began *not* to work when we adjusted the roles of Herod and Marcus to play to the strengths of the actors we had for the last production. Our director always discusses the parts a lot with the actors, in fact the first rehearsals are often spent just talking about them and trying things out, and during the first discussion with the actors playing Herod and Marcus it was decided they would try out the idea that Herod might be going mad: Was he paranoid? Or was he rightly sensing that all this talk of a new messiah might pose a threat to the authority of Rome – and him? At the same time, Marcus was becoming more of a politician, and 'managing' Herod. (We were to cement this alteration by changing his costume: the soldier's tunic, helmet and cape went out; in came a toga for him too.) So far these changes had been made in the way the characters were played, and apart from taking all the 'sirs' out of Marcus' speech, which immediately transformed the balance of power between them, no script changes had been needed.

As the actors and the director discussed Herod's madness, it became clear that the scene needed more lines, and that we also needed to see that, apart from Marcus, Herod was surrounded by sycophants, which would also lead him to mistrust the advice he was getting. We decided 'scribes' could fulfil this role. We would also try swapping two of Herod's and Marcus's key lines to make Marcus more in control. I went away and rewrote the scene, found some willing 'scribes', and after a bit of tweaking in the next rehearsal it ended up as a completely different scene – Herod became an unstable dictator, surrounded by 'yes men', lashing out wildly and panicked into a decision. Now it was Marcus who was reigning him in, limiting the order to 'just the boys'.

The new scene (which became known as 'nought to insanity in three minutes') gave us a much more complex Herod than we had had before and a more sinister Marcus. Herod's shifts in mood contrasted with Marcus's calmness and stillness, and there was much more tension in the scene. But it was only by watching the rehearsal and listening to the discussion that I got an idea of what these actors were capable of, and the sort of effects the director was looking for. Also watching how the rewritten scene worked meant we were able to make final small revisions on the spot.

Physical considerations at script stage

If you are in a purpose-built performance space you should not have to worry too much about audience comfort, except in ensuring your play is not too long. Are you going to have an interval? If so, you need to consider where in the play it will work best. (First acts generally end on a transitional moment – e.g. a new piece of information or event changes the potential for the situation - which leaves the audience wanting to know what is going to happen next. Second acts are generally shorter than first acts, a time-honoured and successful formula.) You may decide that you don't want an interval at all. Our first production only lasted forty-five minutes so didn't require one; it has since grown to nearly ninety minutes and still doesn't have one. This is probably as long as you can expect people to sit comfortably in one place, without a break, however.

If you are not in a theatre, you need to consider how you are going to seat your audience, and it's useful to decide this before you start writing, as it may affect how you can construct scenes. An audience's comfort depends to a large extent on how well they can see what's going on, so you need to consider sight-lines. If you don't have access to raked seating you will almost certainly need to use a stage of some kind. Performing 'in the round' may offer better sight-lines to more people. Be aware of where the aisles will be (health and safety considerations will affect how many seats in an unbroken row you can have, and how wide aisles must be; also you can't of course have seating too near fire exits) and then when you are writing scenes think of the aisles as part of the performance area. A 'promenade' production (where the audience moves from one location to another) is also an approach you might consider.

If you are in a conventional proscenium arch situation, with a curtain, you will need to remember when scripting the play that changes of scenery (if used) take time. You can get round this by:

(a) writing your script with only one multi-purpose set in mind, perhaps with areas which can be differentiated for particular sections of the play

(b) carefully planning where your changes of scene can occur – in a traditional three act play, this could be during two short intervals

(c) using the old pantomime device of having action in front of the drawn curtain, while the set is being changed behind it.

You may decide that you need only a very simple minimalistic set, with only symbolic devices or props to indicate the location (this is what we do). All of this will need to be discussed with the director and designer while you are writing the play, as there is no point you writing locations they will find it impossible to represent, unless you have already thought carefully about staging solutions.

When constructing a community play it is worth remembering that theatre will be just as unfamiliar an experience for the majority of your *spectators* as it is for a great number of your *actors*. The likelihood – indeed the hope – that your play will be performed before an audience many of whom are not regular playgoers (for some it is certain to be their first experience of live theatre) should both inform and be exploited by your production.

People who have not been brought up with theatre as part of their lives are quite likely to have unconsciously formed as many prejudices towards it as people who have grown up in households where, for example, football is not valued, may have against the sport. They may assume it has nothing to offer them and is *for other people*. As it is outside their experience, and having managed perfectly well without it, they may require some persuasion that going to see a play is worthwhile. In either event, the reluctant spectator is often concerned (a) that they will not understand (or care) what is going on (b) that they will (consequently) not fit in and feel out of place and (c) that they will, quite simply, be bored.

The community play needs therefore to engage with the challenge of the reluctant spectator. While the 'buzz' surrounding the production, and the involvement of friends, family, neighbours or colleagues may have got as far as bringing them through the door, you have an obligation to make this a night they will remember. You need to pull out all the stops, and draw on everything you know and feel about theatre, to give your audience an experience they will not only enjoy, but will wish to repeat. Your role, in a sense, is to open a door to a new world, and make it as easy and attractive as possible for them to come in. At the very least, you aim to offer something that will make them feel that theatre is no longer *for other people*, but that it can speak to *them*.

Creating variety – comedy

One way of seducing an audience is by making them laugh. Introducing comedy (if appropriate) early in the play helps an audience warm up and relax and will make them more receptive to what follows. In any case, the most serious plays often have a few laughs in them, and you ought to avoid creating a play that is unrelievedly earnest. At the same time you need to be careful that comedy doesn't undermine the serious intentions of the piece. You will get a feel, as the script unfolds, for where comedy will work. In our play, Herod cracking jokes would compromise his sinister aspect, whereas the Storyteller cements his key relationship with the audience by sharing a witty aside with them; the audience can laugh at Joseph's bewilderment concerning Mary's pregnancy, but we don't want to encourage the same kind of identification with the Angel Gabriel.

You can have a bit of fun with the known facts of your story, rather like in some films set in some earlier period, someone will opine that some new-fangled invention (the telephone, the car, the aeroplane) 'will never catch on'. You can have someone in your local story who everyone knows goes on to do something extraordinary, belittled – along the lines of the famous assessment of Fred Astaire early in his career: 'Can't sing, can't act, can dance – a little.' You can insult the character of the locality e.g. 'The people of Ourtown are known to be an unruly rebellious breed, given to loose living

and low morals…' – for some perverse reason, the people of Ourtown will enjoy that. The only thing you have to avoid with these kinds of references, is it starting to smack of pantomime. An 'in-joke' of this kind is best used when it serves to tell us what a character is like, and shouldn't just be inserted for its own sake.

Wit is welcome at almost any point in a script where it does not undermine the prevailing tone – unless, of course, this is a point you want to make about a character: that they are irreverent or unserious or plain silly. When something funny occurs to you, think about whether it is funny in context, and whether it detracts from the job that scene is doing. Also be very alert to how it goes down at read-through or rehearsal. If no-one else finds it funny, it's probably just you that does.

Most of the comedy in our play is concentrated in the shepherds' scene, and was inspired by the problem of what to do with them. You, too, may find that a sticky patch in the script is where humour can usefully be introduced. The shepherds' role in the play is to be visited by the angel and to then go and visit the newborn baby. I had no idea what to do with them between the beginning of their scene and the point when the angel appears. The only thing I knew I wanted was that one of the shepherds would be more dissatisfied with his job than the others and unable to stand the tedium. He would wish that something exciting would happen – but in fact he would be off-stage when the angel appeared, and would miss the big moment. But that didn't give me a scene. What did shepherds actually *do* when they watched sheep? I racked my brains, and became so desperate that when I found myself seriously considering having them washing their socks by night (as in the bastardised carol) I knew I was in trouble. I decided I would take all the pressure off myself and just start writing about the things shepherds might talk about. There was that enormous star, for a start. Then I had them moaning about the Romans, showing off their limited stock of Latin phrases, wondering about the meaning of life, and, of course, talking about sheep. It started to flow, and before long I had got a scene that would do the job it needed to.

I hadn't set out to write a funny scene, and in fact didn't think it was *that* funny – a sort of gentle humour had crept in as soon as I had taken the pressure off myself by just inventing the shepherds' conversation. However, in the read-through it became very funny indeed, I think precisely because *nothing happens*. In rehearsal the shepherds added in a lot of their own 'Ar's, and their own pauses, while *nothing happened*, which everyone seemed to find hilarious. I quote this example because, despite my earlier, largely valid, injunction, I learnt that you can get too obsessed with advancing the story, and making every line count. If you get really stuck somewhere in the script, try a more relaxed approach, and you may find the characters start speaking for themselves (and even making jokes).

Creating variety – surprises

So your audience will appreciate a bit of comedy; it will enjoy surprises too. These need not be big effects. One of the effects we have used which most delighted the audience was achieved by a very simple device. When flashing back in time to the account of Mary's own birth (to aged parents), fourteen-year-old Mary ran down the long central aisle of the church (away from the stage) and a tiny four-year-old Mary ran back down the aisle into the scene. (Little Mary had no lines – the idea occurred because as the daughter of the actor playing Joseph she happened to be at rehearsal – and she just had to be picked up and hugged by her 'mother'.) All this effect required was to make a matching mini version of Mary's costume. You will find it useful to sit down with the director and designer at various stages in writing the script and discuss where imaginative effects could be used.

Another technique you can exploit when writing the script is planting actors in the audience. In our play, the Storyteller has quite a cosy relationship going with the audience, to whom he explains where and when we are in the story. However, he is not far into his story before there is noisy dissent in the audience which he first tries to ignore but is soon obliged to investigate. The three gossips' heckling, from different parts of the auditorium, ends up in them taking to the stage to give their version of the story.

Sometimes members of the audience are rather uncomfortable when the gossips start making a disturbance and sometimes even 'Shhh' them, before they realise it's part of the play, which is very gratifying (especially to the gossips).

We also plant actors in the audience in the scene where a husband is chosen for Mary. Joseph and the other suitors are ordered onto the stage by the Storyteller, as though randomly picked from audience members.

(We have thought of getting real audience members to come up and be part of the line-up of suitors, but decided modern dress would upset the look of the scene. However, audience participation of some kind might be something you want to think about using in your play.)

The Storyteller disappears halfway through the play, as it takes off under its own steam once all the flashbacks and flashforwards are out of the way, and we thought he needed to be brought back at the end. I had him appearing right at the very end, claiming to have overslept, and needing to be filled in by the shepherds on what had happened. What none of us were aware of, in the hectic atmosphere of the first production, was that the Storyteller was actually having a 'sleep' amongst the audience. We later learnt that when the actor (Ian Ashmeade) had finished his main duties as Storyteller, he would go and sit next to a child in the audience (the audience are in pews, not individual seats, so you can make space), quietly explain (in character) that he was just having a little rest, and that they were on no account to let him fall asleep; he would then, to the child's consternation, 'fall asleep'.

There may be many ways you could use actors in the audience in your play. It is an effective way to keep the audience involved by reaffirming the interplay between the stage and the auditorium and is always a surprise.

Creating variety – spectacle

The scale of your cast will give you the opportunity to treat your audience to visually striking scenes and images – don't waste it! The one thing a large cast guarantees you is the opportunity for spectacle and this is something you must consider and exploit at script stage.

In our own play there were several opportunities for colourful and noisy crowd scenes. We had Rome's dictat (via Herod) that 'all the world is to be taxed' delivered by a Roman soldier in a busy marketplace, so the crowd's reaction could convey the sense that this was yet another unwelcome imposition by an occupying power. Later in the play, we wanted to convey the chaos in Bethlehem where there clearly were not enough beds to accommodate all the visitors who had come to be taxed. Again we flooded the stage with bodies, primed to be tired, hungry and thirsty after a long journey. The scene began with a troubled wail (mainly provided by the children), and Joseph and Mary, at opposite ends of the crowd, had to push their way through the teeming people to reach each other, and indeed, hear each other (only to learn that Joseph had found nowhere to stay). The overall effect spoke powerfully of misery and chaos.

Our venue is the largest building in the village: the biggest of the three churches. Holy Trinity, like many large churches, has a long and relatively narrow space for spectators, making for less-than-ideal sight-lines to the performance area, so to mitigate this wherever possible we have the action beginning the scene from the back of the church and moving forward. In crowd scenes we have the crowd flowing down the central aisle and the two aisles either side, to make the audience feel the action is happening all around them. (The director always makes the point to the cast that the people sitting at the back have paid the same as the people sitting at the front, so we have

to do our best to make the action accessible to and inclusive of them. In fact, the people sitting at the back and middle of the church, while getting a reduced view of the more intimate scenes in front of the pews on the main stage get a far better view of the main 'spectacular' set pieces, which begin at the back of the church and process forwards, and can best be seen in their full splendour from further back; so, it all works out pretty fairly in the end.)

The procession of the Magi has become more spectacular with each production and the addition of music gave it the effect of a true pageant. For once we suspended the rule that everything must inform character or advance the story. Here we were happy to just let the audience revel in the splendour of what was before them. The Magi's procession remains a moment of spectacle, just for its own sake.

The other moment which we intended to exploit visually was the scene of the Adoration. As the script developed, from this tableau to the end of the play became something like a pageant, with very little dialogue and a lot of music. Mary, holding the newborn baby, and Joseph, are dressed and lit like a renaissance painting, positioned at the farthest end of the church (where the high altar would usually be). The choir, offstage, sing, as first the Magi and then the shepherds, in very low light, process down the central aisle and pay their respects. The shepherds explain that they have been told to spread the word, so they might expect more visitors.

By now the main part of the church is in darkness, and every other child and adult in the play come down the three aisles with candles until they are all kneeling, a carpet of little white lights, before the tableau. The singing ends and there are a few moments of a still and silent tableau before the horrified voice of a woman screams from the back of the church: 'Run! They're killing the children! Take your children and run!' The ear-piercing screaming of 140 children as they then run back through the audience is blood-curdling and, according to audience-members, extremely hard to forget.

When the stage has cleared, only Mary, baby and Joseph are left. The director had the idea of bringing the adult Christ, on his way to be crucified, on stage at this point. This extremely controversial image linked the massacre of the innocents with the crucifixion, birth with death, Christmas with Easter. It made sense and was powerful. It also gave us an 'ending', which we didn't

really yet have. From the opposite end of the church, a beaten and bloodied Christ begins the long journey down the aisle, carrying his cross, as a lone voice (out of sight) sings 'Sometimes I Feel Like a Motherless Child'. When he eventually reaches the holy family, he stops and he and Mary look at each other for a long moment, then the lights slowly go down...

We were braced for several controversies about the play. They were: firstly, the inclusion of extra-biblical legends, which do not to the modern eye appear to differentiate between miracle and magic; secondly, our very feisty Mary, who is always played by a fourteen to sixteen year-old girl, and tells Joseph at one point she hates him; and thirdly, this final image of the adult Christ, in a dirty ragged tunic, with blood running down his face from the crown of thorns. In the event, neither the legends nor the young Mary seemed to upset anyone, and the scene with Christ carrying his cross was the most praised image in the play. I quote it here to illustrate the point that spectacle does not always have to involve a vast number of people: it is about the scale of the concept. It also serves to demonstrate that a scene with no dialogue can make a lasting impression.

Finding an ending

The director would have been brave enough to make this the final image of the play, but I wanted a more upbeat ending. We also had a bit more plot to get through, as I wanted to show that Mary, Joseph and the baby escaped. Before I explain this I need to relate one final anecdote about casting changing the script. When we cast the Roman soldiers, they were all much the same – average build and height, except for one who was very tall. Several cast members sidled up to the director during rehearsal, hissing: 'Isn't he a bit tall for a Roman?' It seemed a bit rough to sack him due to height discrimination, so the director asked me to put it in the script. I included a reference to his height in three different scenes. Each reference got a bigger laugh (three, incidentally, is a magic number for a running gag) and that, we thought, was that.

Next I wrote a scene in which Joseph and Mary and the baby (concealed in her shawl) are escaping the massacre of the innocents, but just when they seem to have got away with it, they encounter a Roman soldier. He is standing alone in the 'street', looking up at the star. For reasons the audience can only infer, after taking a long look at the baby, the soldier lets them go, and then discards his helmet and sword as he leaves.

As the Roman soldiers had been pretty undifferentiated it hadn't mattered which of the soldiers was the one in this scene, but of course making him the 2nd CENTURION (the tall one) rounded off that little character beautifully – all the way through he had been different, and the butt of a joke, and then he turned out to be the Good One.

The ending was getting neater all the time. The director had now given in to the inevitability of *The Hallelujah Chorus,* but the problem was going to be how to assemble the entire cast on stage ready to sing without it taking ages and being untidy, distracting and noisy *and* without detracting from the scene that had just happened. I had some dialogue for the gossips in the pulpit, based on an apocryphal story, to wrap the story up, so instead of having them on stage saying the lines, we recorded the dialogue and played it in the darkness, while everyone in the play got onto the stage.

The dialogue related that 'all kinds of fierce wild animals' had approached the family as they crossed the desert into Egypt, terrifying Mary, but the animals demonstrated that they were there to guard the baby and provide a safe escort. It ended: 'They walked among wolves and feared nothing. And the lions directed them in their path.' In the dark this dialogue from disembodied voices seemed much more atmospheric and poetic than it had when declaimed from the stage (another tip worth remembering) and the contrast was all the greater when the lights came up revealing the entire cast on stage, singing the *Hallelujah Chorus.*

At this stage, the director observed that we had already had three endings (the conversion/defection of the soldier; the gossips telling what happened next; and *The Hallelujah Chorus*) but still lacked an Ending. The problem seemed an intractable one, because the narrative *itself* (as it appears in the gospels) doesn't really have a satisfactory ending, as it's told as part of a larger story. So I went away to try and write an ending for a play based on a story that didn't *have* an ending, and that ironically proved to be the key.

As soon as the last chord of *The Hallelujah Chorus* is sung, before the audience have time to put their hands together, there's a shout from the back of the church.

STORYTELLER: Wait a minute! I'm supposed to be in this bit!

He hurries down the aisle, pulling on his coat.

The SHEPHERDS emerge from the crowd.

2nd SHEPHERD: Who's he?
STORYTELLER: I'm the storyteller! This is my story! But I missed the end.
1st SHEPHERD: How can you be the storyteller and miss the end?
STORYTELLER: I overslept. Sorry. But I need to know how it ended.

The three SHEPHERDS join the STORYTELLER at the front of the stage.

3rd SHEPHERD: Oh, it was brilliant. You should have been there.
STORYTELLER: What happened?
1st SHEPHERD: Well, first there was this angel.
2nd SHEPHERD: No, first there was the star, *then* the angel.
STORYTELLER: Another angel?
2nd SHEPHERD: Well, I suppose it could have been the same one. Then some wise men.
3rd SHEPHERD: And us!
1st SHEPHERD: And a few other people…

The four of them continue talking as they walk down the aisle towards the back of the church.

3rd SHEPHERD: Yes, but we were really important.
STORYTELLER: So, how did it end?
2nd SHEPHERD: With a baby being born.
STORYTELLER: That's not much of an ending.
2nd SHEPHERD: Oh, it's not the end. It's just the beginning.

And they're gone.

Just as the opening of your play should captivate the audience, your ending should somehow release them. Avoid multiple endings, but make sure all your storylines are tied up and that we know or can guess what has happened to all the major characters. Whenever possible, leave the audience on a high.

Copyright – a word of warning

If your play is adapted from a book, you must ensure you are not in breach of copyright. Using history books as references is of course fine, but if you have modeled your play on a novel (especially if you have lifted chunks of dialogue), or very closely on one piece of published research, you must both credit the original author and ensure you have permission and have paid any necessary fees. Look into this before you start, as you may not gain permission, and exclusive stage rights may already have been sold. Copyright exists until seventy years after the death of the author (in the case of joint authorship, seventy years after the death of the last surviving author). In other words, if it is seventy years since the author's death, you can do what you like with their work.

This also applies to music – it is very easy to breach copyright without intending to when including music in your script. For example, let us say you are depicting 19th century rustic revels and choose to have the well-known song 'The Lord of the Dance' performed in the scene, believing it (as many people do) to be a traditional hymn/folksong. In fact the song was written in 1963 by Sydney Carter (now deceased) and you would have to seek the permission of the copyright owners (in this case, Stainer & Bell in the U.K.) in order to include it in a public performance.

Unless the CPA is willing (and has the resources) to pay to perform a song that is in copyright, you will be wise either to use music that is out of copyright or to write or commission your own songs. (The Choral Public Domain Library on the internet is a good source of free music.) It may be that you can persuade the copyright holder to let you use their material free of charge, and while you may be lucky, this is unusual. Copyright in a musical work is not infringed by incidental inclusion in your play (for example, it is playing on the radio in a scene, or someone is humming a snatch of a song) but deliberately including whole musical works (e.g. a song) in the play, with or without words, for which you do not own copyright, is illegal unless you have negotiated a license to do so.

There is also the copyright of the script itself to consider. If the writer is formally employed by the Community Play Association and paid to write the script, the Community Play Association, and not the writer, may retain the copyright, unless there is some agreement to the contrary in their contract. If the playwright is writing the script (or the composer is writing the music) for no fee, and there is no contract, the copyright automatically remains with the artist, and if the script (or music) were published, unless the writer (or composer) reassigned the copyright to the CPA, the writer (or composer) and not the CPA, would be due royalties.

Whether you are a hired writer or writing the script for free as a member of the community is bound to influence your approach. In either context, you will need to dig deep and think very creatively about how you can make your script *serve* your community play group. This means making opportunities for your cast to communicate their story in a way which is a credit to them and is a rich treat for the audience. It's a big responsibility. Be realistic, but don't be afraid to be demanding (in the script). Once rehearsals have commenced, be flexible when you can, stick up for what you believe to be crucial, and above all remain a constructive part of the project throughout the process.

Experienced playwright, Charles Way, offers some insight into the process and some tips for writers new to the Community Play:

> I have worked on three large scale community plays that have involved a core body of professionals (a director, writer, designer and project manager) and a large number of community participants. The key thing is to find professionals who really understand and believe in the nature of the work, who know that the process is as important as the product. Without a good, healthy relationship between the professionals and the community then it really won't work.
>
> In the mid 80s, I was asked to write a play for the town of Monmouth. The idea came from active local people who had seen other community projects. At our first public meeting there was some scepticism about the project, not to say hostility, but through a combination of open workshops, a small but significant group of locals got committed to the idea. This is important and the project mushroomed from there. The resulting play, *Bordertown,* with a cast of about sixty plus orchestra was performed in the local church and sold out for ten nights. It took almost two years to create and after initial training workshops, the script

became the 'binding agent' – the focus which allowed our project to really gather pace. Twenty years later, we had a *Bordertown* reunion which shows the deep effect such a project can have on individuals and a community as a whole.

Community plays need not be as large and all-consuming as the one described above. Every other year local professionals in Crediton Devon lead an al fresco Shakespeare production performed by a local cast. Each year the standard gets higher and the audience following grows. The key seems to be clarity of purpose. Why are we doing this project? What do we wish to achieve? Once the project is over, there needs to be an honest appraisal. Without this, a community play can be a one-off event that has no lasting effect on society, rather like one of those dreadful 'Garden festivals' that used to take place in deprived areas of Britain.

The community play is neither amateur nor professional – it is a hybrid affair and therein lies its potential problems but also its power. Everyone learns – not least the professional because they are involving themselves in the reality of lives lived, not merely reflecting them in an art form. When one goes to see a community play or project one witnesses far more than 'art'.

Tips for writers:

1. Writing a play for a large cast can be a great release after years of being asked to write for three actors and a puppet. There are dangers however. The first is one of control. Key to this is to be true to the story you're telling and the characters in it. In other words don't try to please everyone in the cast – you will let them down in the end.

2. Be prepared to explain your central premise – the why of the story again and again and again. This will pay dividends.

3. There may well be a large number of smaller roles. Make sure that each of these is well defined and it will give satisfaction to the actor.

4. Don't assume that the local participants can't act and therefore write in a simplified manner.

5. Make use of theatre in its totality, harnessing choral speech, music and movement as ways of telling your story and involving large numbers of people.

6. Involve the community in your research, and possibly in the writing process itself. Work through practice rather than theory. Many will enjoy and learn from the re-writing of scenes etc. what makes the play better than in the previous draft.

7. Be full of praise, and encouragement. Only from that base can you then begin to challenge the artistic effort and take the cast with you.

•

5. Casting and Rehearsing

Although a community play tends to begin as the obsession of a single person (or two, in our case) and it needs one or two people to drive it along the whole time, it obviously requires the support and input of many more at other stages. First of all, you need to sound out a few key people about your idea – by 'key' I mean people who have a lot of contacts in the community already; people who know the community well; people who are good at getting things done; and people who are enthusiastic about community projects. As explained earlier, I got the three village ministers on board first; then I lobbied the Head of the local primary school and got his support and co-operation. We talked to a lot of people and asked them to talk to other people they thought might be interested. We did not hold a meeting until we had a draft script, so people could get an idea of what they were letting themselves in for. (If I had been doing a local historical story I would almost certainly have had the meeting before script stage.) Although there were many posters up advertising the meeting, the thirty or so who came were mostly people we knew or people connected to those we knew. As the script was fairly short (and a lot of it is music) we were able both to read through the play, with various people reading various parts, and cast a lot of the principal parts on the spot, as well as discuss how it was going to happen.

Casting and directing adults

Gaining people's confidence is of course vital and the director most of all must gain people's trust. In our own case, the director and I are both writers (in 'real life') and we had originally planned that we would co-write the script, that he would direct and I would produce. (As it turned out, he had a lot of work on that year and I ended up embarking solo on the script, though many of the images and ideas were his.) In any event, people seemed to feel we could be trusted with the project and it was helpful that the director had directed professionally – this gave people confidence. Some of the people who came to the first casting session/meeting had been involved in the village panto; a couple were fairly experienced amateur actors, but many had not done any kind of performing since their schooldays.

Different community plays have different approaches but we think it is important not to hold formal auditions, but a casting session instead, where people can try out different parts and not feel under the same sort of scrutiny and pressure where you try out for a particular part, in competition with others doing the same. We had already decided that anyone who wanted a speaking part would get one, and we would write them if necessary.

When recruiting a cast, you need to cast the net widely. The whole point of a community play is to involve the community, and that means reaching well beyond 'the usual suspects', such as members of amateur dramatic groups. People with some experience of performance will be extremely useful, but your production should not be dominated by these, and you may well find yourself having to 'undo' their learned habits. (For example, amateur actors used to working on a conventional stage may need more assistance in feeling comfortable performing in the round than people who have never picked up some of the theatrical conventions associated with the proscenium arch. Regular amateur actors may also find the whole ethos of the community play rather different from what they are used to.)

This may be a good point at which to give an insight into what it is like to get involved in a community play as a participant. John Shippey came to the Haddenham Nativity in 2003, with a great deal more theatrical experience than most of our actors. This is his insight and experience:

> The first experience of participating in the Nativity introduced me to a new way of working in the theatre. Yes, there were certain governing parameters such as the script and some of the key images which had been developed and proven in the 2001 production, but beyond that the director's approach was very flexible – suiting action and development to the ability and experience of the actors, but always stretching and encouraging. This meant that the production felt almost like a 'work in progress' right up to the final rehearsals, but it gave it the vibrancy that I had seen as a member of the audience and it brought out the best in all those involved.

> After my first involvement, while I was keen to take part again, I didn't really want to take the same role (John the Baptist), so, in 2005 I became Marcus the Centurion, in 2007 the Second Shepherd and in 2009 Joseph.

This most recent role involved not considerable, but certainly significant, changes to the text as I was taking over from the person who had played Joseph in all four earlier productions and I was a good 20 years older than him. This made Joseph a father- (grandfather-?) figure to Mary – an obvious change from the previous productions, but a relationship that is supported in the source material and one which the writer was happy to represent – and it provided me with a fulfilling role and a new insight into a story with which I thought I was wholly familiar.

Throughout my involvement with the Haddenham Nativity I have experienced and enjoyed its inclusivity and adaptability; its valuing and acknowledgement of the individual without losing sight of the importance of the whole. I believe that these attributes must be major part of its qualification as a Community Play and what makes it so effective.

While it is a huge bonus to have the support and participation of experienced players and lovers of theatre like John, you need to attract participants from those factions of your community who are not predisposed to come along. Your publicity must reach those people. If you have already established links with some groups, you can use them to help disseminate publicity. So, for example, if a local school is participating in some way (from lending or letting rehearsal space to providing child performers) providing enough copies of your publicity for one to be sent home with every child will reach a great number of households. Posters need to go up in shops and pubs, leisure and sports centres, and anywhere else people will see them. Get help to distribute flyers to passers-by in the local market, in the high street on a Saturday. The local press will be most effectively used if you can interest the editor or an individual journalist in your story; local radio is also an efficient way of reaching a lot of your target group. Make time for personal approaches for these. You can also approach local organisations, from the football club to the W.I., and encourage them to circulate your information. Most local organisations will have an e-mail database of members, and you can ask for your publicity to be forwarded to a great number of potential participants this way.

What does your first wave of publicity aim to achieve? Are you inviting interested people to a meeting or to get in touch with you? This initial approach must be carefully worded and needs to make it abundantly clear that *no experience is necessary*. It is a good idea to make a general approach from the outset: make it clear you are looking for people not only to perform, but to help with costumes, props, set-building and all the rest. Sometimes people may feel comfortable enough to come forward and offer to assist with a backstage aspect of the production, and, when they get more of a feel for the production, subsequently feel emboldened and that they actually *could* perform after all.

Posters/leaflets/flyers are all useful, but in specific situations a letter can produce the best results. When recruiting children for our play we send a letter home to all parents through the local primary school, the bottom third of which is a slip which they are asked to complete indicating *whether or not* they are interested in their child participating and *giving permission* for them to do so, by a certain date. Killing two birds with one stone, we also ask parents whether they might consider being involved in any way. On that certain date we collect all the slips from school and then have a ready-made database of potential child participants (name, address, contact phone numbers, child's class) as well as parental permission (otherwise it will be necessary to go back and write to all the participant families again to get this). Hopefully we will also have recruited some parents. We can also see who has said 'no' and there is no point pursuing *and* who hasn't responded at all, who may be worth pursuing.

The local school of course will not pick up all children. We have a low participation of teenagers, probably partly because this is an age of high self-consciousness, but also because our teenagers all go to secondary school out of the village. We always send publicity to the drama and music departments of the local secondary schools, but have had virtually no take-up from this. You should get a better response for this age group if you have links (personal or formal) with a local comprehensive.

One problematic group is reaching children who are home-educated, as these are largely invisible. For our first Nativity we picked up one such family, who came to us through the local Baptist Church. The family consisted of Mum and five children, the eldest of whom was fourteen, the youngest a small baby; all six were in the play (Dad worked for the USAF nearby, which was why this American family found themselves in an English village). As rehearsals progressed we learned that the children were home-schooled as a result of their parents' objections to the school curriculum here; most importantly, they were Creationists and did not want to subject their children to being taught the theory of evolution. Their children did not mix much with other children from the village except from the Baptist congregation. For them, participation in the play offered a social experience which was otherwise inaccessible. The whole family made new friends as a result and became more integrated into the life of the village.

In terms of a social and theatrical experience, is clear that the community play has even more to offer children who are home-schooled than other children, and it is important to try and reach them and their families. Many children who are educated at home – perhaps most – are not linked with churches and it is actually very difficult to find them. It may be that this group uses the library more, for example, so make sure your project is advertised there.

Depending on the demographic of your area, there will be different cultural or ethnic groupings where you might expect take-up to be low. Make these groups a real priority and allow time for personal approaches. Offer to go and explain the project in person and exploit any personal contacts you and your team may have. You may also choose the devious route – a number of our actors over the years have claimed to have been tricked into being in the play, but didn't seem to mind. For the first production, we had most of our principals by the end of the casting session, and picked up all the others in the first month of rehearsals. The father of the girl playing our first Mary made the mistake of arriving early to give her a lift home from rehearsal and ended up being persuaded to read in for the Storyteller – a role he has now played in all five productions. We had no Roman soldiers until the director recruited some drinking mates from our local pub to come and move some furniture in the rehearsal room, then asked them to stand in a couple of scenes as 'the Romans hadn't arrived yet'. By the end of the evening they had agreed to be Roman soldiers, and to recruit some more mates.

We would never, I think, have managed to recruit such blokey blokes without the director's willingness to resort to such underhand tactics: these men would *never* have come to a casting session. Although they agreed to be in the play, they said they wouldn't wear 'frocks' or make-up. It was therefore a source of some amusement to see them at the dress rehearsal in their short

tunics, advising each other on the best sort of fake tan to rub on their legs. One of them researched and taught the others details such as the correct salutations and they generally became a gang, built the set and provided support whenever we needed muscle. They were also excellent Roman soldiers. Once they realised they just had to be themselves being Roman soldiers they were utterly convincing and responded amazingly well to being given little bits of business, such as casually waving away imaginary flies while they were on duty. Everything the director wanted the Roman soldiers to do, he told the actor who was playing Marcus (the soldiers' senior officer in the play) and Marcus gave the orders. Here is a lesson about working with the dynamics in the group.

Planning rehearsals

There are two principal ways of planning your rehearsals. The first, and most usual, is to have dedicated periods for rehearsal which are the same times and days each week (e.g. Wednesday evening, Saturday afternoon). Draw up a list of all these rehearsal dates and also include run-throughs, dress rehearsals and technical rehearsals. Circulate this information at the casting stage or as early as possible and give the cast a deadline by which to get back to you about any of these dates they can't make. This will quickly reveal whether some cast members are simply not going to be able to attend enough rehearsals to be able to participate and will save much heartache later. It will also show you whether one of your rehearsal times is so unpopular that it is not going to be worthwhile, so you can rethink the schedule.

The other way, which we use, is to circulate to the cast an empty potential rehearsal diary – this includes all the times you could possibly have a rehearsal – i.e. the director or musical director is available and a rehearsal space is available – and get them to fill in the ones they could or couldn't make. Again you must give them a deadline for completing and returning this. (To save time, we also circulate a form for their measurements for costumes with this – getting two jobs done in one go.) Against this you need a list of which characters are required in which scene, and by combining the two sets of information you can arrange to rehearse particular parts of the play when everyone in that section is available. This has to be done very quickly, so that dates for which a performer had been available do not get booked up in the interim, and then immediately circulated. You will need to make it clear that this schedule has been carefully planned around the performers' declared availability so they must now stick to the dates when they are required – these should now be fixed dates in their own personal diaries.

When planning rehearsals be aware of which parts of the play may require more rehearsal than others and build this into the schedule. Always plan more rehearsals than you think you need – some may be cancelled for unforeseen reasons – and you can always cancel a rehearsal that does not later seem necessary. Your schedule needs to include the date, time and location of the rehearsal (make the latter very clear if your rehearsals use more than one venue). It is also helpful to indicate in the schedule at what point you expect performers to be off their books – i.e. to have learnt their lines. The schedule should also include useful contacts – especially a mobile number for the person who they need to contact if they are going to be late or unable to come to rehearsal. Performers need to understand that just not turning up at rehearsal means people are waiting around unnecessarily.

People not used to learning lines may need tips on how to do this and reminding that they need to know not just their own lines, but their cues from other actors. Encourage actors to help each other learn lines by getting together outside the rehearsals. (Our three shepherds, for example, get together to record their scenes on tape or voice recorder and then use the recordings to learn their lines while they drive to work, etc.)

You will also need someone to be following the script at rehearsals and able to prompt actors if they forget their lines. It's a good idea if the same person does this job each time, so they are aware of where there are deliberate pauses in the dialogue. If you are having a prompt for performances, they must be totally familiar with the way the script has been rehearsed. Our director makes it clear from the outset that there will be no prompt at performances as he feels when an actor takes a prompt it 'breaks the spell'. If actors get into trouble onstage they help themselves – or each other – out of it, without breaking character, or letting on that things are not going quite according to plan. Reassure performers that the audience do not have a script in front of them and are usually blissfully unaware when things don't go exactly as rehearsed.

You will increase any anxiety your performers feel at the beginning of rehearsals if you are using a language they don't understand. At the first rehearsal explain the following.

Blocking – working out where the actors will move and position themselves onstage – involves certain terms to help the actor understand where the director means them to move, or face. These include:

Downstage – the front of the stage, nearest the audience

Upstage – the back of the stage, furthest from the audience.

These are easy to remember if you bear in mind raked stages, which slope downwards towards the audience, giving the audience on the floor a better view of the action on stage.

Stage left – the actor's left, as s/he is facing the audience

Stage right – the actor's right, as s/he is facing the audience

The fourth wall – an invisible, imaginary wall between the actors and the audience. (A realistic set of a room, for example, may suggest the back wall and two side walls; the fourth wall is where the fourth 'real' wall would be.)

You will know how much else you need to explain, and do tell the cast to feel free to ask questions at any point about anything they don't understand.

In the schedule, make it clear what the following terms mean:

Run-through – the whole play will be run through, from beginning to end. (You might want to indicate whether this will be a 'stopping' rehearsal, dealing with problems as they arise, or a rehearsal 'without stops', regardless of what goes wrong.)

Dress rehearsal – a rehearsal as if it is a performance, with full costume and make-up. Performers should expect this to be 'without stops' unless the director has indicated otherwise.

Technical rehearsal – a rehearsal primarily for sound, lighting and special effects but where the cast is required. This may be a dress rehearsal with stops. Actors should not feel this is purely for the technical crew's benefit – their own cue to come on or go off may be a lighting cue, for example. Actors should be prepared to be patient as often the same sequence may need to be gone over several times.

Ons and offs – a rehearsal in which only entrances and exits are covered. Doing this ensures people can physically get from A to B (for example, if they go off through one entrance and come on shortly afterwards from another) in the time allowed, and is extremely useful when a very large cast is involved. It reveals where there may be bottle-necks backstage, or at stage exits, or where a particular manoeuvre is taking too long and needs to be re-thought.

Remember that people are giving up their precious leisure time in order to be part of the play. Don't call people for rehearsal and then not use them. Don't direct the irritation you may feel about certain cast members not showing up for rehearsal at the ones who have turned up. Consider, halfway through the rehearsal whether you still require all the actors who are present. If you are not going to need some of them again that night, let them go home.

It is good to include some rehearsals where you have everyone present (or as many as you can) throughout the schedule. This helps people get the bigger picture. Just as the director should make time to drop in on the odd band, choir or dance rehearsals, the choreographer, musical director, lighting and sound technicians should be encouraged to visit acting rehearsals – especially the 'big' ones.

Your stage manager or his/her assistant needs to be present at rehearsals to make sure any furniture used in the set is in the right place and any props are present. If you are not rehearsing in the performance venue it is important that the actors have a sense of the actual space they will be performing in, so the stage manager should mark out the dimensions of the 'real' stage on the floor and indicate where entrances/exits are.

Always make sure rehearsal rooms are left as you found them (i.e. remove tape or chalkmarks from the floor, put furniture back, don't leave dirty coffee cups or rubbish). Whether you're paying for the room or not, you do not want to give your production a bad name by leaving a mess. If anything gets broken, for example, immediately inform the venue's management and offer to recompense them. If there is a caretaker, take care to maintain a good relationship with him/her. Don't let rehearsals over-run if this is going to inconvenience the caretaker – s/he may well not be able to lock up and go home until you have finished. Don't let the importance of what you are doing, blind you to other people's needs and priorities. A large stock of goodwill is one of your most precious commodities.

Rehearsing successfully with people unused to performing depends on creating the right atmosphere. People have to feel comfortable and supported, but you also need to establish rehearsal etiquette. The director or producer needs to explain at the outset that actors not being used in a scene are welcome to watch the rest of the rehearsal, but talking will distract the actors. (Ideally, provide another room where tea, coffee and conversation can be made.) Decide how your rehearsals are to be structured: do you want a formal tea break? (We tend to not have these, as time is at a premium, and people go and make a drink when they can, but if your rehearsals are long ones they can provide a welcome respite and also an opportunity for the actors to get to know each other.)

As far as getting the actors to interpret the characters goes, directing is the same whether the actors are professionals or not, the only difference being that non-professionals will need more encouragement to relax and 'go for it'. Allow them to move when it feels right, at first, rather than hampering them with rigid blocking, and where possible go with the moves they make. Encourage them to try out different ways of playing a scene, so that they feel comfortable with the script and see it as a tool rather than a daunting obstacle to be surmounted. If you have time to do some workshops before rehearsals proper begin, this can be very useful in helping people lose their inhibitions about performing. Talk to the actors individually (not in front of everyone else) when you can about their parts. Above all, make them feel you are absolutely confident they can do it. You should find that an *esprit de corps* is soon established and that actors will support and appreciate each other.

That's all the positive stuff; now to the negative. You may find actors telling each other 'how to do it'; wanting to rewrite lines; having issues with the script – all of this has to be firmly resisted (unless, as sometimes happens, these are real improvements). If you make sure you are approachable (before, after, or during a break in rehearsal) you will avoid a confrontation during a rehearsal. Be understanding about the fact that people will have some problems – and don't dismiss them. Listen, and if you can, solve the problem, or assure them that it isn't a problem. There is a lot of value in saying that you see what they are saying, but you have reasons for wanting to try it this way for now – often the problem, once aired, will evaporate. As long as you are listening to people you will avoid factions or deputations. You can't direct by committee: directing is about creating a benign dictatorship and also being a bit of a Machiavelli.

The principal fear that people have when new to performing is that they will be somehow exposed or made to look 'silly'. You need to reassure them that it is in no-one's interests – including yours – for this to happen and you won't put them in that position. My final tip is the old praise sandwich (which should really be a criticism sandwich, as that's the filling). An actor is doing something badly: you praise something about the performance, then address the problem, then praise them again. (It sounds patronising, but many people naturally do this without realising it is a strategy.)

Casting and directing children

Involving children may not necessarily involve any extra budgeting and, in fact, tends to have quite the reverse effect, because, crudely expressed, children also represent bums-on-seats. In our experience, the participation of a single child has resulted in up to twelve ticket sales, when the whole extended family has decided to turn out. By involving children you also have a new raft of potential 'helpers': parents. Parents can be recruited to fulfil all kinds of roles, from making costumes, to supervising children in rehearsals, through working backstage during performances. You may even recruit adult cast members or technical crew this way, who you may have missed through your other publicity efforts.

So, children add value on many levels. They also add fun.

In terms of logistics, the easiest way to involve children is formally *en masse*, for example through a local school or a youth group.

As explained earlier, once the village ministers were on board, we secured the co-operation of the head of our local primary school. This was easy for him to agree to, as he was about to leave! Fortunately, his replacement was very keen on the idea and saw it as a way of forging and reinforcing links between the school and the wider community, whilst giving the children the opportunity (possibly once-in-a-lifetime) of taking part in a large theatrical production. We decided we could only accommodate children from Key Stage 2 ('juniors' in old money), as we felt it was unfair and unrealistic to expect children under seven to be able to cope with the challenge. Over the ensuing five productions we have found this to be a sound cut-off point.

For the first production, the whole of Key Stage 2 of the school was recruited *en masse*. This was 140 children. It was actually too many (though we didn't realise this at the time) – for our play, anyway – and the catch-all policy meant there were a number of children who didn't really want to be there and there was not enough for them all to do, so they got bored. We coped and the children worked very well under the circumstances but we decided subsequently to have an opt-in rather than an opt-out policy. Since then we have invited all children in Key Stage 2 to be in the play. Anything between forty and sixty volunteer; between thirty and fifty usually stay the course. (Always recruit more children than you need. Parents often agree without realising the play clashes with another activity and children themselves can get cold feet.) We learnt a great deal about managing children in the play during the first production.

The first tip is to rehearse the children separately from the adults for as long as possible. This has several advantages:

1.) The adults are not spooked by the inevitable chaos, or apparent chaos, which can characterise early rehearsals with children. *You* can be prepared for it to seem hopeless at first, but you can't afford your adult cast to feel doubtful about other elements of the production outside their control.

2.) The children will be quite accomplished by the time the adult players see their contribution. This helps with your adult cast's confidence in the whole project, and the children benefit from the positive reaction they will get.

3.) The adults will be quite accomplished by the time the children see *them*. This tends to be the first moment when the children begin to realise they are

part of something big and impressive and it helps them to see that they are
an important part of an important thing. They will finally understand why
everyone can't stop while they go to the loo, etc. and they will start to take
responsibility for themselves, their props, etc. They start to get the bigger
picture and their role in it all begins to make sense and becomes something
worth doing well.

The second tip concerns keeping the children focused. Time is usually at
a premium and you will want to make every minute of rehearsals count.

Your greatest enemy when preparing children for performance is flagging
concentration. This takes a variety of forms, and comes from a variety of
causes, all of which require strategies to address them. Ideally, you want one
or two people whose exclusive responsibility is the children's participation,
and an agreed approach. A trained and experienced teacher would have
handled the children much better than I did at first and I learnt, and continue
to learn, to take advice from teachers on how to gain and sustain children's
attention, and recommend that you too consult teachers – or better still, get
a good teacher on board.

You have to go into children's rehearsals expecting and understanding that
children will talk or play at any available opportunity, and you do have to lay
out your stall from the very beginning, in terms of the behaviour you expect.
You can begin to make life easier for yourself by minimising the potential for
distraction. An empty space (such as a drama studio or an empty room) is
ideal. However you may not have much choice in your rehearsal venue. If you
are in a church hall, where there is a white elephant stall laid out, for example,
children will feel obliged to examine all the items minutely – so tell them at
the beginning that this is someone else's space and we (use 'we' as much as
possible, rather than 'you') mustn't touch their stuff. Similarly, a school
classroom is not ideal, as it is full of stimulating things – again, explain from
the outset what is off-limits. Do not give young children pencils and pens
unless you want them to poke each other with them. Hand out things
necessary for an activity to be immediately undertaken and collect them up
as soon as they are redundant. If handing out instruments (say, simple
percussion), make it clear *before you distribute them* that they are not to be used
until it is time to use them. Even an adult cannot pick up a tambourine

without shaking it, so be patient, but if a strict look or word doesn't work, have an offender hand the instrument over to you until it is time to play. It is an old saw and a true one that children get the message by example.

Be kind, be cheerful, be welcoming and be polite. At the stage of early rehearsals children will have little concept of the scale of what they will end up participating in, however much you explain it, and their relationship with you will be more important than their relationship to the project. Try to learn as many of their names as you can (it is very easy to discover that you know the names of the extroverts – and especially the distracting extroverts – without trying, so make an effort with the co-operative majority). Children are generally less inhibited than adults, but you may still find that some boys are reluctant to sing, for example, and some children who want to perform will come out with tiny inaudible voices. You have to build their confidence. Children thrive on praise, so congratulate them whenever you can. If you have had to tell a child off, look for the next opportunity to praise the next good thing he or she does. Even a frown carries far more weight with a child who you have praised than a child you have not. It is also as important to be polite to children as it is to adults – we expect 'please' and 'thank you' from them, so show them the same respect.

After a couple of rehearsals, children will begin to feel they have a relationship with you, and may begin to share things at inappropriate moments – for example, you may ask a question to check they have understood an instruction, a myriad of hands will shoot up, the child you pick to answer will then tell you that their cat had kittens last night. While the impulse to share such intimate experiences with you is to be treasured, any encouragement will lead to more pet-related contributions from other children, and before you know it, it's time to go home. Similarly, as the production becomes more real to them, they will start to ask questions about costumes etc., often in the middle of a rehearsal. Make it clear that the last five minutes of every rehearsal is specially reserved for news and questions – you can then defer any unrelated interjections until then.

The third tip concerns what is dressed up for adults as 'rehearsal etiquette', but for children is good old-fashioned discipline, and is largely noise control. Your children will be used to a variety of authority/teacher styles (some may have a shouty teacher, others may have a strict but calm disciplinarian, others may be used to a teacher who tolerates a certain amount of noise but no more) and you will have to establish your *modus operandum*. Try to avoid shouting (although this is very tempting when there is a real racket in progress). Shouting makes you look discomposed – and if it doesn't work, you have nowhere higher to go. How you establish conduct at the first rehearsal is extremely important.

1.) Be in the rehearsal venue early, so you are there when the children arrive. If the children are there first, you will walk into a room that is already noisy.

2.) Make sure there is somewhere for everyone to sit – this can be the floor, but make sure there is enough space for children to sit without squashing each other.

3.) As the children come through the door, ask them to leave their coats and bags by the door or at the back of the room (less to fiddle with) and then to come and sit down.

4.) When you reckon most have arrived, if there is still too much noise for your voice to be heard, put your finger to your lips. Most will understand this – if they are looking, and the chat should subside.

Your first rehearsal will involve you explaining the project and their part in it. Invite questions, and establish the 'hands-up' rule – most children know this from school. Choose something to rehearse that you think they will enjoy, and where a satisfying outcome is easily achievable. There can be a significant drop-out rate from children, so you don't want to put them off at the first rehearsal by doing anything too complicated. Aim for them to leave looking forward to the next rehearsal.

The fourth tip is to get the children used to certain forms which will be useful when they are involved in full rehearsals with the rest of the cast and the performances themselves.

In our own case, there is only a tiny backstage area, so when the children are not onstage they are sitting to one side of the auditorium, where they can be seen by the audience (if they turn their attention away from the action, that is). It is therefore vital that they are still and quiet when they are not performing. They also need to move around the building unobtrusively and quietly, sometimes while scenes are in progress, to be in the right place for

their next entrance. For this reason they need to be able to take mimed instructions, which, of course, they can only take if they are looking at you. I pinched a strategy I had seen a teacher use to quiet down a noisy classroom. He puts his hands on his head, which the children understand to mean they should do the same *and* stop talking. One by one, the children did indeed do the same and the last child to see the signal was understandably a bit embarrassed. I established this as my signal for quiet at children's rehearsals (again, avoiding shouting) and it became invaluable when I needed to attract the children's attention in busy full rehearsals when there was a lot of other noise and activity going on. During performances they knew not to copy me, but if they saw me put my hands on my head they knew to focus on me and watch for an instruction. Fortunately, children seem to have a herding instinct, so as long as a few children know what you are asking them to do, the others will follow.

I have mentioned the advantages of keeping the children separate from the main cast for as long as possible, but the principal benefit is that, being unacquainted with the rest of the action, they will naturally be quiet and attentive when they *do* see the rest of the play, as it will all be new. Having children involved from the beginning means they will see the play a number of times and will begin to get bored both during late rehearsals and performances, which becomes very difficult to manage, especially when at this stage there is so much else that needs doing. We now have an absolute maximum of three full rehearsals with the children and the adults together, and as few as one of these might be a complete run-through. As a result, they watch the parts of the three performances when they are not on stage very quietly and attentively.

A practical consideration which also makes sense of the separate rehearsal system is that it is very difficult to find a time when both children and adults *can* rehearse together. Weekends seem ideal for this, but people of all ages are often busy then. People returning from a day's work can't usually begin rehearsing before 7.30 or 8pm – many children of primary school age are getting ready for bed at this time. A good way to integrate the adults and the children later on in the rehearsal process is to have some overlapping rehearsals: for example, having children from 6.30-8pm and adults from 7.30-9pm. Planning the rehearsals so that the scenes involving everyone fall into the half-hour overlap can resolve this difficulty. While discussing time, you need to be aware that parents will not tolerate children being involved in a lot of late nights. The best times for children's early rehearsals are in school during the lunch-hour, or immediately after school. Keep evening rehearsals to a minimum, and spread them out. We even avoid having our dress rehearsal the night before the first night, as this means children are getting to bed very late four nights in a row. As it is, having been up late for the first two performances, some of the children are clearly tired by the last night.

Rehearsing during the school lunch-hour may sound less than ideal, and of course you can only do this if you have someone to take these rehearsals who can make time during the day (a teacher or a parent working from home is ideal). However, little-and-often is often more productive with children. I found that more seemed to sink in during two half-hours a week than was retained from weekly one-hour rehearsals.

When you first rehearse with the children in the performance venue, you will need to sit them down and give them a talk about the next phase. This will include pointing out hazards in the venue and 'no-go' areas. They will need to understand that they must be quiet when they are not being used and be ready to follow new instructions. You will be handing them over, in a sense, to the director, so introduce him or her. Explain that there will be props and costumes lying about that they must not in future touch (I let the children have a good look at all the props on the prop table at this point, allowing them to touch and hold them also, to get any curiosity over with. Everyone wants to finger the Magi's gifts, but John the Baptist's head on a plate is always the clear favourite.) As they also use props, ask them to imagine going to fetch their prop for their entrance and finding it is not there. That is why no-one must touch other people's props. Let them explore the venue and then get them all on the stage to finish off your chat.

Finally explain that from now on there will be a lot of people at rehearsals and there may be people sitting in the audience sometimes. They (the children) can begin to practise what they will need to do in the performances themselves, which is to think of the stage as an enchanted island, where the people on the stage can only see each other and the audience is invisible (i.e. if they see their mum in the audience they must not wave at her). This will keep the magic of the play working (you explain) and make the audience really believe the characters and the story.

This may all seem a bit much, but children do need this to be spelt out, and they do observe the convention if it is explained to them. As with all the above advice, it will seem extremely patronising to people used to handling groups of children, but may be helpful to those who are not. You will also be bound to discover and develop your own methods of child management, so these are just guides.

Finally, if it is possible for the writer to spend some time with the children, or liaise with the child-handler, this can be very helpful. Children will focus most when they have a creative input, rather than are just doing what they are told. If there are places in the script where children can be creative, do exploit it. In our own play for the scene when the crowds pour into Bethlehem for the census we got the children in groups to write little scripts for what they would be saying (children of course are excellent at complaining about journeys so they did a great job) – they also had to write a part for an adult, who would be part of their family group. They enjoyed doing this, and then enjoyed teaching the adults their lines, and it meant that the opening of this scene was full of the babble of family groups all talking at the same time rather than unconvincing ad-libbing.

The Artistic Director of London Bubble Theatre Company, Jonathan Petherbridge, offers some useful insight into working with both children and adults in community theatre. He speaks about his recent work with London Bubble on the *Blackbirds* project, a play about the experience of Londoners who lived through the Blitz:

> London Bubble worked towards the performance of Blackbirds for over sixteen months. It brought together a number of substantial elements – participants of all ages who had worked with Bubble for a number of years, the stories of local elders who lived through the Blitz in South East London and Bubble's track record of making inter-generational and site-specific work with, and for, its local community. The company successfully applied to the Heritage Lottery Fund for support to train children to interview elders who had been children themselves during the Blitz. I then

led workshops to develop the testimony into images and scenes before we employed a writer (Simon Startin) to shape the testimony and the ideas that had emerged from the workshops into a script. We then rehearsed the script for four months.

Blackbirds was finally delivered as an inter-generational performance piece given by forty performers in a local disused church and was attended by elders, children and residents keen to hear about what had occurred in nearby streets within living memory.

I've directed quite a few community pieces and particularly enjoy working outdoors with inter-generational casts. Why outdoors ? Well, it's healthy and demands energy, you can create detailed characters as well as fun choric images or sections of what I call 'patterned movement' with groups of ten or twenty people of differing shapes and sizes – check out Pina Bausch or Rosemary Lee. Why inter-generational ? It's fun and gives energy, individuals develop respect for people from different age groups, learning is passed, children may lead and adults may learn from the young. All of which leads to a healthy and strong dynamic which is detected and enjoyed by the audience.

My advice – try and work with the same community on a number of different projects, allow a culture of theatre making to develop, make work about the community performed by the community to be given back to that community. Remember theatre works on a human scale, locally and socially.

Rehearsing a community play choir

Our community play choir is led and conducted by Cathy Priestley. She has this advice on the subject:

Working with a scratch choir is exciting and scary, challenging and fulfilling. There are differences between a specially gathered community choir and other choirs, and some of the differences took me by surprise. Like many aspects of the community play, this is a learning experience for the leaders as well as the participants.

The volunteers for the first Haddenham Community Nativity choir were a very mixed group. There were some experienced singers (not all from a choral background) but the majority had never sung as adults. Some people knew each other from other areas of life but many were apprehensive about trying something new among a group of strangers. Very few of the singers read music, and the mix of voices between parts was unbalanced (even when the individuals knew which part they were best suited to sing!). We also had to contend with varying levels of commitment, interest and availability, with some people thinking that they only needed to attend occasional rehearsals and others who were seduced by the call of an acting role. Later in the rehearsal period we also had to contend with those who wanted to sing but not move around, learn the music off the copy, wear costumes or sit on the floor.

We managed to address all the concerns with more or less success. As we had considerably more female singers, we found or arranged pieces for Soprano, Alto and Men (rather than the traditional SATB). Some pieces also had an additional line for children (who learnt their parts separately at school and joined the adults at the end of the rehearsal period). For a couple of pieces, the men were unavailable (being Roman soldiers), so the singing was provided by a three part (SSA) women's chorus. In order to help those unfamiliar with singing harmonies, we also held some additional sectional rehearsals as needed.

A few tips to anyone tempted to put together a community choir:

1.) Get together early with your musicians, especially if you are using a multi-part band rather than just a keyboard player. A choir who can sing perfectly in rehearsal on their own are likely to be thrown into silence or chaos by the sound of instruments. Similarly, make sure the choir are familiar with the space they will be performing in.

2.) It is a mixed blessing being ambitious in the choice of pieces. If it comes off, you will have something really wonderful on your hands, but you need to be flexible enough to substitute if something really isn't working.

3.) Make sure you schedule in a couple of music-only rehearsals late in the rehearsal period. Music that seems to be working well can fall apart when people are standing/sitting/moving in unaccustomed places, so you need an opportunity to revisit the music after they start participating in full rehearsals.

4.) If, as we are, you are not in a warm environment, or are outside, even grown-ups can need telling to wrap up under their costumes. More than other performers, the choir will probably spend quite a lot of time sitting still in one place and will not produce a good sound (or be a happy choir) if they are shivering.

Rehearsing and managing musicians

The earlier musicians can join the main rehearsals, the better, but this is often not possible, especially if a large band or orchestra is involved. The following tips apply to a group of musicians of any size.

If it is going to be important that the musicians can see the action on stage, this has to be thought about and organised at the beginning, when planning the use of the performance space. Often only the musical director or conductor can see the performers – but they must be able to see them. A monitor can sometimes get round this, but it's not ideal, and if the actor giving the cue happens to stand in a different place, or if there is a technical problem with the monitor, there is no way out except guessing the cue. If instruments are not augmented by microphones, having the musicians facing the stage will considerably reduce how well the audience can hear them.

If they are facing the audience, they cannot, of course, see the actors. Having them in front of, and to one side of, the stage can work well. If they are in a traditional orchestra pit, of course, the conductor is their only guide.

Because the musicians know only their 'bits' they will not be familiar with the whole piece or know how their contribution fits in. If you can run to scripts for the musicians, this can be very helpful. If not, they will need a list of cues. It is not helpful to give musicians one line of dialogue as a written cue. A digest of the action, followed by a few lines of dialogue, gives them time to prepare to play and also helps them understand when there is a quiet moment in the show and their moving could be distracting.

When planning your rehearsal schedule you will need to allow extra time for when the actors and musicians come together and not expect any more from those rehearsals except marrying these two elements. You do not want to waste the limited time you have with musicians by using these rehearsals for anything else.

Don't assume musicians will supply their own music stands and lights – establish who will be providing these well in advance as they may be difficult to procure at the last moment. Battery operated LED pinlights which clip onto music stands are invaluable – they provide good light for the musicians to see their script/cue-sheet and music, but don't spill light elsewhere, and avoid yet more trailing cables. (These are also very useful backstage, if in a venue where backstage light may spill onto the stage.)

It is vital that the musicians do not come as a last minute surprise to your sound technicians! Make sure they liaise from the beginning and that the sound designer has the opportunity to hear musicians in the venue in good time to plan any augmentation – either for musicians or singers. Finally, if you are paying musicians, the preferred form is in cash, before the final performance.

6. The Production

This section deals with practical and technical aspects of the production itself – costumes, props, lighting, sound, special effects – and includes contributions from the people responsible for these aspects from our own production.

Costumes

You will need to get help with these as early as possible. Ideally, you want to recruit a wardrobe mistress or master from the outset who will relieve you of the burden of responsibility for costumes while consulting regularly with you. Hiring costumes is expensive, so unless you have a decent sized budget for costumes you will be making them yourselves. Here is the advice of our wardrobe mistress, Gina Keene, who has costumed many other productions besides ours, and also runs a costume-hire business from her home.

Costuming a community play can be incredibly rewarding, creative and satisfying, but is initially daunting. By its very nature, a community play will have a large cast. The first thing you need to do is build your confidence. Trawl the internet and consult books on costuming for ideas and inspiration. I find children's Ladybird books with their clear and colourful illustrations can be a wonderful inspiration for anything historical or fairytale.

Inspiration is all very well, and absolutely necessary, but you have two tyrants at your door: time and money. There is never enough of either of them! Establish what your budget is as early as possible, fight for a bit more, and then work out the proportion you are going to allocate to each costume. Are you going to use the same amount of money for each character or are you going to spend a little bit more on the principals and slightly less on the chorus? It is worth having a list of every character (chorus/crowd/extras' included) with a pencilled-in budget against each of them: then what you overspend on one, you can 'claw back' from another. However, it is vital that you are flexible with this. The common, and quite reasonable, understanding is that the principal actors will get a larger share of the budget and the chorus less. But a chorus has to complement the principals and is an essential part of the overall effect, so it is important that the 'lowliest' member of the cast (as if there is such a thing) is dressed with as much care (if not as much cash) and attention as the star of the show. If any member of the cast is close enough to the audience for them to notice a dazzling nylon zipper in a 16th century costume, or trainers on a 19th century child, this is somewhere as much money, or time, or thought, should have been spent as on the leading lady.

The sensible side of me wants to advise: don't spend a penny until you know what you have to spend, but the differently-sensible side of me says: if you see a useful bargain, grab it while you can. Try to see a ridiculously low budget as a wonderful challenge. There are quite a few sources of cheap materials and clothes that can be transformed into costumes. As soon as the play starts to get publicity, make sure an appeal for fabrics and things you might want is included in appropriate publicity. For example, for the Haddenham Nativity, we want any plain (i.e. one-coloured) cloth (curtains or bedlinen, even towels), striped cloth, anything woolly or furry (for the shepherds), old sandals (to be dressed-up for the Roman soldiers), anything exotic and sparkly (for the Magi), bits of leather (general), lengths of material with which to dress and drape the set, and so on.

We have actually very rarely had to buy brand new fabric from a shop to achieve our ends – but then we have saved enough by scrimping and saving on other things to be able to splash out on something really fantastic when required. You can make a list of things that will be useful for your

production that people may well be chucking out and make it easy for them to be donated – i.e. give a phone number and offer to collect. Try following the example of many charities, who do a leaflet drop (get the fundraising support group, if there is one, to help you) appealing for stuff. Make one side of the leaflet a brief explanation of the community play project (clear this with the fundraiser, so your appeals don't clash, but harmonise) and make the reverse of the leaflet a clear large print label they can leave on a bag on their doorstep on the day you have said you will collect, so you can identify it. (Avoid designating the day the rubbish is usually collected!)

Jumble sales are sadly so much rarer than they used to be, but are always worth going to. (Tip: don't take each item up and ask the price; get a bundle of things and then ask – you'll always get them cheaper.) Charity shops and resources like the Emmaus Community (Google them and find your nearest by typing in your postcode) are also good. Make sure the cast is aware of your needs; put a card in the post office or similar; ask people in highly visible locations to put a sign in their windows; ask the W.I. and other local organisations to mention your appeal at their next meeting...it never hurts, and costs nothing, to ask.

The most unexpected donations can be extremely useful. For the first Nativity we were given by a member of the cast a huge pair of blue (real) velvet curtains. Not only were these in excellent condition but, unusually, the lining was also blue. This one donation gave us enough fabric to make a warm velvet cloak for Mary's procession round the village (and 'the flight into Egypt'), but the lining made Mary's dress (and, for one production, mini-Mary's dress) and what was left over was used as stage dressing for certain scenes. When looking at useful length of fabric in charity shops and jumble sales, always look at the reverse side. A design that can appear too severe and modern on one side, can, on the 'wrong' side, especially on woven fabrics, look 'older' and more authentic – effectively a faded, worn version of the proper side. Remember that your cast is unlikely, in their character, to all be wearing brand new clothes. If you have a lot of poor or working class characters, they mustn't look as if they are wearing their Sunday best (unless, of course, they are supposed to be wearing their Sunday best).

Dyes used to be a cheap solution to many problems, but are now comparatively expensive. However, balance this with how cheaply you are getting the material. For example, if you are lucky enough to acquire ready-made items, very cheaply, which are the right style and size but the wrong colour, dye can be extremely useful. Similarly, fabrics which are the right design, but the wrong colour, which you may have been lucky enough to get free, are worth the money spent on dye to make them useful. Modern dyes can be easily used in a washing machine these days without ruining it, but do follow the instructions. Cramming more fabric in than the dye is created for, just leads to disappointing results and wasted money on the dye. However, it's worth being aware that any synthetic content in the fabric will most likely mean that the dye won't 'take'. I still have some delightful pale pink fabric (once white) that we tried dying scarlet for the Romans.

You will need to work closely with the director and designer (if you have one) early and regularly on costume design. There is no point spending hours getting a costume to your satisfaction if it was never going to be what was wanted. Make sure you have a clear understanding of what is required, and early on make your suggestions and advice known. If you haven't costumed for the stage before, it is a good idea to talk to the lighting person about the colours used. Pale colours, beige say, can just look white under lights and navy blue can look black. Make sure you know in what lighting context the particular costumes will appear.

A note on practicalities. As you are dealing with performers who have other jobs, there is every chance that they will be performing after a day's work. Somehow they have to have a journey from work, sort out their home life and prepare themselves in the short space of time between working and performing. As this often doesn't allow time to eat, all manner of food can enter the dressing room. All these – and tea and coffee – can be disastrous for costumes. Make it clear early, and often, if necessary, that you do not want to see anyone engaging in anything that might damage or stain costumes (necessarily involving you in extra work). No-one can help accidental damage to their costumes, and should be encouraged to come to you with any problem straight away, but make it clear that anything which could cause damage is not welcome near the costumes. Similarly, unless you have fire-proofed costumes (this is pretty simple, and requires only a special spray) reiterate any warning about fire hazards, especially if any naked flames are used in the production.

In professional productions (e.g. on a film set) it is part of the wardrobe's role to take care of actor's comfort off the set (e.g. providing robes for actors

in near-nudity; providing coats for actors between scenes shot outside in cold weather). It may be as well that you take on this role, in terms of clothes, too, in case no-one else has thought of it, if you are in a chilly environment. For example, in our Nativity, the adult Jesus wears only a thin tunic for his scene, and has to sit through over an hour of the play before he is required, in a very cold church. We have a special

'Jesus coat' for him, and have blankets strategically placed for actors who are not wearing a great deal and have long chilling periods of waiting between their scenes. In outdoor productions you should be prepared to make similar provisions, unless someone else has covered this. If you have actors going barefoot, have a rug for them to stand on when they are not on stage.

Similarly (a lot of being involved in a community play means taking up the slack – if you realise no-one is doing a particular job, and you care enough about it, just assign it to yourself unless anyone objects), I would consider it my role to remind actors not to wear anything personal that might be anachronistic (e.g. watches) or inappropriate to their character (e.g. wedding rings). Your director or designer will be the one to make a ruling about whether spectacles are admissible, but you may be the one who has to remind the cast.

One common error with 'crowds' or any group of people is to have them in identical costumes. This is fine for pantomimes and formal choruses in musicals but militates against realism in this kind of play (unless the characters are being used in a symbolic way, or really would have had uniforms, for example). A bunch of butchers look much more like real butchers if some have longer aprons, some have short ones (and both look like they have seen some action) and they have different head-gear, and different shirts. As long as they are all identifiable as butchers, your job is done. If they all look identical, they don't look real.

In the Haddenham Nativity, our first production was necessarily the most expensive regarding costumes, as we were starting from scratch, whereas we now have an extensive wardrobe, which usually requires only a few things to be made, or adapted. We don't rest on our laurels, however, but use that luxury to go to town on particular principals, such as the Magi, who we redesign each year, and other roles which may have undergone change – or just because we've had a great idea, or acquired something we want to use. I also quickly realised in that first production, given the scale of the task, that it is sometimes more efficient to hire than make costumes. It would have taken me more time and more money than we had to make impressive costumes for the Roman soldiers (who really cannot look as though they are in fancy dress), so we hired them, and their real metal shields and swords, and they looked fantastic.

The Magi represented a different kind of challenge, as we wanted them to look all-of-a-piece without looking as though they were all made from the same pattern. We go to town on the costumes of the Magi on every production, and find different ways of keeping a theme uniting them, while they all look individually glorious. Sometimes they are black and gold – in other incarnations they have been red and gold; citrus colours; blue and silver.

Try to get the actors in costumes before they 'have' to be, so you can watch rehearsals and see if anything stands out incongruously. Ask the director to call for a costumed rehearsal while you still have time to make changes, alterations and improvements. I would only add that you will always do well to delegate. Get parents to help with children's costumes, for example. Many cast members may be willing to make their own – just make sure they have a clear idea of what you want. Never turn down an offer of help! Most importantly, establish early on a relationship and a clear line of communication with the director and designer. They may have ideas that you don't think will work – the only way to find out is to try them.

While the general public will admit to knowing little, if anything, about directing, lighting, sound or set design, everybody knows about dressing themselves. After all they do it every day and some spend hours in shops getting the 'right' look. Therefore members of the cast do have an opinion about their costume. It's all part of the creative process of putting on a play (which our director would call organic) that things evolve. Some ideas from the cast about costume are valid and helpful. Others, sadly, are way off the mark and it requires a combination of gentle firmness and tact to deal with this. What seems perfectly reasonable to them might not fit in with the overall vision which, of course, they don't know about.

Last, but far from least, remember that actors can have valid reasons for feeling very sensitive about their costumes. If somebody really has problems with their costume, don't make it a point of principle that you won't change it. They might have a personal reason that you don't understand or need to know (it reminds them too forcibly of the gown they wore when being treated for cancer in hospital; it does not accommodate a colostomy bag; it is difficult for them to take on and off if they need to go to the loo frequently, etc.). Be accommodating, be understanding, put yourself in their shoes. Finally, before each performance make sure you see (or someone you trust sees) every individual in their costume and, when you are satisfied, don't forget to tell them how great they look.

Costume design

One way you can get the most out of inexpensive costumes is by a judicious use of colour. Our director and our wardrobe mistress came up with a colour system which immediately gave a distinct feel to each scene. Red was inevitably going to feature in the Roman soldiers' costumes, in their helmet plumes and cloaks, so Gina made this a theme for all the characters associated with the Roman occupation: Herod, Herodias and Salome all have red in their costumes. This lends a richness and an exotic, if sinister, atmosphere to Herod's court. By contrast, John the Baptist, who is brought before Herod at the beginning of the play, wears a dirty white shift, so instantly looks out of place; there is also structural patterning to this costume, as it is similar to what the adult Christ is wearing at the very end of the play.

Our director wanted Mary and Joseph to be as instantly recognisable as the traditional images associated with them, so Mary was in blue. He also insisted that she was the *only* character in blue. This was extremely effective

in crowd scenes, as the audience could always pick her out, and emphasised the idea that she was 'special'. The exclusive use of one colour for a major character is a strategy you might find useful, especially if you want the audience to be able to easily identify that person when there are a lot of bodies on stage and a lot going on.

We similarly excluded pure white, however little of it, from any costume, as we were reserving this for the Angel Gabriel. (In the event, we came up with another solution entirely.)

Producing a lot of costumes on a tight budget makes absolute historical authenticity very difficult; what is achievable, however, is an *impression* of authenticity. For example, the vast majority of our cast wear what we call 'basic biblical', which is a look informed by old children's books about Jesus or epic films like *Ben Hur*. To try and produce historically accurate clothes would probably be less acceptable to the audience who recognise the convention of 'basic biblical' costume for what it represents. Our costume designer decided that all the ordinary people (the majority of the cast) would be dressed in 'autumnal hues', so they are in all shades of brown, deep greens, ochre, mustard, claret and burgundy. This, for some reason, 'looks authentic', and though there is perhaps no historical reason why some of them shouldn't be in yellow or turquoise or pink, such colours would stand out inappropriately. The main thing to remember is that you don't really want the audience to *notice* the costumes, in the sense that they start thinking about them. What *looks* right is often more effective than what may technically be more accurate.

Small details can also make a big difference. All the women and girls in our play wear headdresses and it is amazing how just a strip of fabric carefully draped transforms a woman in a converted duvet cover into an authentic Nazarene. (It is often forgotten that before the Second World War almost everyone wore some kind of head-gear most of the time – whether your play is set in the 17th century or the first half of the 20th, hats, caps and bonnets will instantly transport the audience to another time, while usefully disguising 21st century hairstyles.) The right footwear can also be extremely expensive if you are going for total authenticity and you often have to go for what doesn't look wrong, rather than what is absolutely right.

Another way of getting round the expense of costumes is to think creatively. When we were planning our first Nativity, we had to start work on the costumes before we knew whether we were getting any funding. The Roman soldiers were the biggest headache, as we felt we really ought to hire these costumes to make the soldiers look sufficiently impressive. Our director came up with the idea of putting the soldiers and Herod in modern day military uniforms, which we could get hold of for a fraction of what the Roman costumes would have cost. The crowd's costume, he reasoned, was timeless and still characteristic of much of the Middle East, and using modern soldiers' battledress would emphasise the sense in which the themes of the story, and particularly the idea of the occupying force, resonate today. As it turned out, the money arrived and we hired Roman costumes, but this would have been a viable alternative and would have made an extremely powerful statement. Modern day dress is an option you might consider in any case.

Unless you have the luxury of somewhere to store costumes that is handy both for rehearsals and performances, once a costume has been made and tried on and found satisfactory, give it to the actor and make him or her responsible for bringing it to rehearsals and performances (the same goes for personal props). If you are using period costumes, encourage the actors to wear them at rehearsals as much as possible, so they get used to managing long skirts, or wearing swords, for example, and moving naturally thus encumbered. Before every performance the wardrobe mistress or master should cast a critical eye over each actor (ideally, get the actors to do it for each other) – a bit of Velcro showing on a Victorian dress, or a label poking out of a medieval peasant's jumper, breaks the spell in an instant.

The other thing to remember about costumes is that they are not going to be worn as much as everyday clothes – and possibly never again – so they don't have to be extremely well made. You also need to resist people's natural urge to look their best: if your characters are 19th century street urchins, you don't want them turning up for the performance with glossy, just-washed hair and beautifully clean, neatly pressed pinafores. If you want their costumes to be dirty or crumpled, you will have to make this plain.

Unless you have a sewing room or a costume store close at hand, a small table equipped with needlework basics is invaluable for last minute repairs or adjustments. A good supply of buttons, safety pins, elastic and hairgrips is also always useful. Sharp scissors and needles are essential and Gina has needles ready-threaded in various colours to save time in emergencies.

Props

Props can be hired, borrowed or made. If you have someone who is willing and able to make all the props, they need to consult regularly with the designer and director. There are few things less conducive to good relations than when a property that has taken someone hours to make is rejected because it's not what was wanted. If you don't have an individual supplying all the props, holding a prop making session (especially if you have to make a number of identical props) can be a lot of fun as well as an opportunity for bonding. Set aside a Saturday or Sunday when you and the props assistant will be around all day and let the cast know, so people can pop in for an hour or so and help out if they want to. An opportunity to play with papier-mâché, glue and paint is a rare one for many adults and this is one of my personal favourite

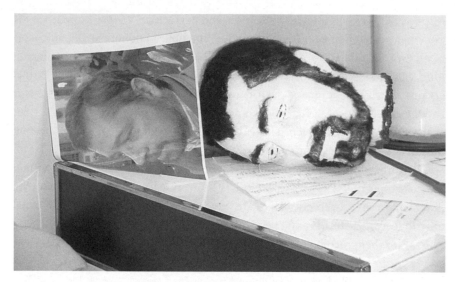

community play activities, partly because you get to see another side of your actors (and I guess they also see another side of you). It is worth being aware that because people (including you) are occupied with a low pressure task, this is often a time when they may air anxieties or problems about the production which they might not want to 'bother' you with at other times. Use the opportunity to listen. There may be rumblings of which you are generally unaware and things which might be causing difficulties that have so far been invisible to you. You may be able to dispense reassurance on the spot or resolve to sort out some of the issues that come up.

Individual actors may volunteer to have a go at finding or making their own personal props. Never discourage this, unless you have a plan already in action, but make it clear exactly what you envisage. However, opening the doors to other people's creative input on fronts like props can be risky but may also throw up pearls.

A tale of two props

When writing our play, when Joseph is chosen 'by God' to be Mary's husband, I had looked at two extra-biblical accounts which vividly described how this choice manifested itself. In both versions, Joseph is among a number of men brought to the temple for this purpose. One source had the temple suddenly filling with doves, who ignored all the other suitors and settled on Joseph, on a staff he carried and on his head. (This I knew we couldn't stage, although it is a symptom of the 'can-do' philosophy that I did actually think about it – could we sew or stick birdseed onto Joseph's costume? Did anyone know anyone with homing pigeons? How would we get rid of the birds at the end of the scene? The clear insanity of this option quickly revealed itself.) The other source had the staff Joseph was carrying bursting into flower, as a blossoming branch in springtime, when Mary touched it. Much of the symbolism of the extra-biblical legends has pagan/fertility aspects and this idea was most appealing and the effect seemed achievable. So that was the one I put in the script.

We discussed constructing the magic stick, as it was known, on the principle of a magician's bouquet that pops out of a wand or a sleeve, but using several bouquets, so that one minute it was an unremarkable brown stick, and the next large colourful silk flowers and leaves appeared all over it. We didn't (and still don't) have a dedicated prop-maker, but the actor playing the priest had made some excellent moving props for the village pantomime so he had a go at this. Unfortunately it proved too cumbersome to operate, the stick had to be too thick, and it looked like what it was: several bunches of magicians' flowers concealed in a tube. The actor playing the Storyteller (Ian Ashmeade), also very clever at making things, had another idea – he could make the stick light up. Problem solved, we didn't think about the stick until the dress rehearsal when it appeared. Ian showed the actor playing Joseph where the switch was, and at the duly appointed moment, Mary walked down the line of suitors, each of whom was holding a staff which looked the same as Joseph's, touching each of them in turn. As she touched Joseph's, a 'harp flourish' was played and the stage lighting dimmed simultaneously. The stick lit up, but not at all as we had expected. Ian had clearly used a set of multi-coloured Christmas tree lights, adapted to battery-power. Worse, they flashed on and off to some pre-programmed manic rhythm. The stick looked ridiculous, particularly because of the dramatic build-up, and the cast fell about laughing.

We asked Ian if he could change the lights to white ones that didn't flash, at least, at which he looked crestfallen. The magic stick had taken him all day to make. The battery and all the wires were concealed under yards of electrical tape and then several layers of paint, so it looked like the other suitors' sticks. He could probably make another one for the second performance, but he'd already taken a day off work to make this, and...basically we were stuck with the garish flashing fairy lights for the first night.

On the first night I was inwardly cringing well in advance of the magic stick moment. Then came the dimmed lights, the harp flourish, and the awful let down of the multi-coloured twinkling stick. The on stage cast dutifully gasped in wonder, which seemed to make it even worse. But then a great wave of laughter rolled back through the church. For whatever reason, the audience loved it and it seemed to be one of those moments when everyone connected. What we had forgotten, of course, was that the audience had no idea what was supposed to happen, or that anything would happen, and what seemed to us a rather rubbish magic stick both surprised and delighted them.

I now think that Noah's dove-on-a-string all those centuries ago could easily have produced the same effect: that the audience understood the point of the prop, and while utterly recognising its artificiality, appreciated the charm of the idea, albeit crudely executed. This audience generosity is a unique feature of the community play: not that they will accept any old rubbish, but that they will take an idea to their heart, and appreciate that it is done for *them*.

The flashing multi-coloured magic stick has survived every production. The other prop we should have thought about long before we actually did was Jesus' cross. Our first Jesus happened to be a carpenter, so offered to make his own cross. The first cross he turned up with was only about as tall as he was, so the director sent him away to make a bigger one. The next one was much more hefty, but he could carry it without much difficulty, so was dispatched to make a yet bigger one. When he arrived at rehearsal with the third cross, he staggered under its weight; the director duly declared it 'perfect'. This was just as well, as we later discovered he had been lugging each cross (too big to fit in his car) up the hill from his home to the church on each occasion, much to the bemusement of passing motorists. Again, if we'd been more specific in the first place, we could have saved him a lot of time and effort.

So, be clear in the first place, check on progress and be grateful. If it is obvious that funds are tight, people are usually happy to donate the materials they use and buy to make their own props, but always offer, and be prepared to reimburse costs, from the budget. This kind of generosity (similarly with costumes), is a nice extra and certainly not to be taken for granted. If you think a prop may prove expensive to make, establish the parameters of cost (what the budget will stand) in advance so there is no embarrassment on either side.

Lighting

Whoever is doing your lighting will need to understand and be sympathetic to the unique demands of the community play. We were fortunate in having a friend, based locally, who runs his own theatre service company. Robin Emery quickly identified our needs, was adaptable, inventive and committed to the idea of adding value to the play by using striking and atmospheric lighting effects. Here he gives his own reflections on the challenges peculiar to lighting a community play.

When I was asked to provide lighting for the first Haddenham Nativity Play back in 2001 I was prepared for the challenge, having already had experience of putting on shows in cathedrals, public parks, warehouses and a range of other unlikely venues across the country. Approaching an event of this kind is pretty much the same as any other theatre piece, except that you have to remember that nothing can be taken for granted. For me, the purpose of lighting is not only to illuminate the actors but also to provide an environment for the action and create some kind of reality for the piece. In a sense, when you work in a non-theatre environment there is a lot more to work with than there might be in a traditional black box theatre space, as you are often able to enhance the existing architecture or natural surroundings, creating effects that can add to the overall stage picture.

The practicalities of working in non-traditional venues are complex and a logical approach is required to bring everything together. It's a bit like running a venue and then presenting a show at the Edinburgh Fringe. First you need to build the space, often transforming a meeting house or café into a performance venue, before actually putting your show on your stage.

Theatre lighting design can often be a mix of what might work aesthetically with what is possible practically and within budget. Broadly, this is the essence of theatre production, which has been described as the art of achieving an artistic vision within the realms of practical and financial possibility. Working in a theatre, you decide what you want to

achieve with lighting and what equipment is required to get you there. The problem with non-theatre spaces is that there is usually nowhere to hang the lights, nowhere useful to plug them in and often not enough power in the building to drive the system. So, power and position can often determine what is achievable.

The community plays I've worked on with Sarah and Leslie have been played in a large village church. Luckily, this particular church has recently had the mains power running into the building upgraded to be able to run electric heaters to keep the congregation warm: useful for our shows, as we have been able to divert some of this power to supply our lighting rig. (You might have to consider a generator, or 'borrowing' power from some other source, if your available supply is insufficient, so you need to check this at the earliest opportunity.) The downside, though, is that the church remains a very cold building for us and the audience and as nativities tend to take place in winter, we are constantly trying to keep warm enough to actually do some work! (As we cannot run lighting and heating at the same time, we heat up the church before the performance; during the show itself the residual heat and the heat from the lights keeps the environment tolerably comfortable.)

Despite the fact that there is more power than usual available, it is still extremely limited, and the socket outlets are in completely the wrong places for our needs. So a great deal of cabling is required to get the outlets to where they need to be. The last incarnation of the show required about a kilometre of mains cabling, all of which had to be carried into the building, laid, used, then re-coiled and returned. A labour intensive process, to say the least.

Having brought in enough metres of cable to provide power in the right places, as well as power distribution and dimming, the second biggest challenge is to provide hanging positions for the lights. In our case this was achieved with the very kind assistance of a local scaffolder, who not only built the complicated stage we needed, but also put in bars, ladder beams and uprights, tied into the fabric of the building, from which we could hang our lanterns, as well as using ground support lighting stands where we could. We were even provided with a purpose built lighting gantry way above the heads of the audience to use as a position for the lighting desk and follow-spot.

With such large amounts of scaffolding and lighting equipment being strewn around the building, as well as a full sound system with around a dozen speakers to even out the sound, it was vital to plan the production schedule so that cabling, scaffold structures and the like could be laid in before the stage was built, so that all the nasty technical bits were kept safely out of the way of performers and audience.

As in any public space, health and safety matters were always at the top of our list of priorities, and method statements and risk assessments were prepared and we were required to liaise with the Church and other authorities to ensure that they were happy that we were staying within the bounds of safety. Licensing laws in places of worship are different to those that apply to many other public buildings, so we were required to provide emergency lighting and lit exit signs for the duration of the event, as they are not required in a church as a matter of course.

As I have outlined, there is a list of practical issues to be dealt with before the more creative work of 'lighting the show' can begin. Another item on this list is the rehearsal process. By their nature, community plays involve working with local people who have their own lives to lead, which can mean that rehearsals are often erratically attended and timetabled, particularly if children are involved.

It is often the case that the first time the entire cast comes together is on opening night. This can present a challenge to everyone, not least the creative team. As a lighting designer, it is key to develop a strong working relationship with the director, as it is highly likely that you will need to light the show 'blind', without most of the actors being there, and refine this quickly and effectively when they are actually on-stage. You need to develop a sixth sense and shorthand to communicate with, as the director is often required to work with the actors at this important time, rather than deal with technical matters. Many a late night has been spent refining a design after a rehearsal, to get it ready for the following evening. Most theatres are dark inside, so lighting can take place at any time of day. In a church – and many other venues – you need to wait for darkness to fall outside before lighting has any real purpose. This again has to be borne in mind when planning your time.

So, all in all, it's important to know what you want to achieve, take nothing for granted and work quickly and effectively with others. Overall, though, be adaptable. These kinds of events are meant to be fun and bring people together, so make sure that happens, if you can. And always try to enlist some useful helpers!

Sound

We were again extremely fortunate in having a personal friend who has his own sound services company and has over thirty years' experience, ranging from West End productions and chart-topping vocalists to student showcase performances. Good quality sound is often overlooked in non-professional productions until it is too late to do much about it, so here are a few helpful words from Roy Truman.

'Theatre is a co-operative art: a combination of co-ordinated artifice to aid the suspension of disbelief. Even a solo performance, dependent on size and scale, can be enhanced by judicious use of light and sound.

The size and complexity of a sound system for an event is inherently dictated by the scale and ambition of the production, the environment within which it takes place, and the (usually ominous) budget. Smaller events (e.g. local amateur dramatics' pantomimes and plays) can be satisfactorily serviced by a knowledgeable and enthusiastic amateur with a relatively small amount of equipment. More ambitious productions (e.g.

musicals) would often benefit from professional input by a local specialised supplier or by being staged in a local theatre. A project like a community play, however, is such an unwieldy animal, that I would recommend the participation of a professional theatre sound designer and operator and an assistant (this can be a proficient amateur).

It is the case with both lighting and sound that the competence and professionalism of the designers/operators do not merely affect the technical aspects of the production, but assist in generating a reassuring technical bedrock that enables the performers to focus on their performances. In an event like a community play it is particularly important that performers feel supported, rather than spooked, by sound and lighting. It is not only what the audience can hear, but what the performers can hear, that needs to be considered, especially when sound sources can be coming from different parts of a venue, and not just from one stage.

The adoption of a flexible, organic approach to a community event in a non-purpose-built venue, as outlined by Robin Emery above, is equally pertinent to sound. As early as possible a consultation between producer, director and sound designer should define how sound is to be utilised in the production – i.e. 'know what you want to achieve' – and the budget available. The next step is a production meeting at the venue with producer, director, set, lighting, sound and stage management personnel, the purpose of which is to decide and co-ordinate the basic requirements of the production – i.e. 'work quickly and effectively with others'.

The sound design for the Haddenham Nativity is quite demanding, having to accommodate a very mobile cast, which uses (and has to be heard in) all parts of the auditorium as well as the stage; a choir that is sometimes singing offstage, and sometimes onstage, and sometimes on the move; many sound effects and much recorded music. Because Leslie (the director) wanted the piece to have the feel of a film, as much as of a play, with scenes leading seamlessly into each other, the sound has to complement this by providing an almost continuous soundtrack, and recorded or live music is often used under dialogue to enhance atmosphere. In addition to this, in order to give a sense of place, speakers are placed in many different locations. For example, when Herod (on the stage, in front of the audience) orders his soldiers to admit the Magi, they march down the aisle to the back of the church and the recorded sound of great doors opening, and the roar of a crowd outside, most effectively comes from speakers placed there, so the source of the sound is consistent with where the great doors (which don't exist) are. As Robin mentioned, one of the difficulties is finding places to hang all this equipment, which is where Shaun Craft, the local scaffolder, was a godsend, as he was able to erect bars, ladder beams and uprights, tied into the fabric of the building (lots of useful pillars and ledges) quickly and safely pretty much wherever we wanted them.

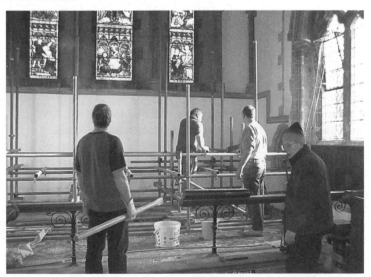

As the sound expert on the play, don't only consider the sound effects dictated in the script, but do contribute ideas which may strike you about where sound could enhance the atmosphere. Some effects may need to be made up especially for your play, by splicing and layering several effects (especially if your writer puts in things like SOUND FX: MASSACRE OF THE INNOCENTS). If you haven't got what you want, be creative with what you have got – for the crowd roar mentioned above I use a recording of a crowd at a racetrack, but you would never know it wasn't Jerusalem, 1B.C.

It is advisable to attend rehearsals in the venue whenever possible to assess any speech reinforcement problems. Many non-professional performers can project effectively, but some, especially younger members of the cast, cannot overcome their small voices and you will need to be prepared to reinforce these. You may also find bits of action are re-blocked, or script changes are made, over the course of rehearsals, which mean you have to rethink how the sound for that scene was going to work.

If you are using portable radio-microphones which have to be shared (i.e. handed from actor to actor), when you do your sound plot, try to arrange it that men pass over to men and women over to women, so that they can rummage around in each others' clothes with less embarrassment. On this subject, you need a fairly discreet swapover area (we contrive this by screening off a corner of the 'dressing room' with two rails of costumes, and having a table with the numbered radio-mics on, so handovers can be completed quickly and in a calm atmosphere).

A final practical point: Robin made the point that you need darkness in order to use lighting; by the same token you need silence to work with sound. In the last days running up to a production it is important to make sure there will be times when people will not be making a noise in the venue while you are working – again, this often means working at night.

The overall design of the sound system is very much determined by the initial aims of the production tempered by the practical limitations identified in the early meetings and rehearsals. This kind of production is always in some sense unique, so keep an open mind and consider various solutions, however unconventional. There are no rules – apart from those of basic physics – that govern sound amplification and reproduction, which is where the knowledge, experience and instinct of the specialist comes into its own. Invariably compromises will have to be made, in every area from source (speech, live music, replay music and FX) to loudspeaker (power, placement, visual intrusion)...always! Just try to identify those with the least impact – an approach that should be deployed through every stage of the project.

Special effects

There are two special effects in our Nativity which demonstrate how you can capitalise on the peculiarities of a particular venue and how a seemingly intractable problem can be resolved with a little creative thinking.

Our seemingly intractable problem was our angel. Because we had gone for a realistic style of dialogue and performance, how could we make the Angel Gabriel seem 'other', or not human? Could the angel have a halo and how could this be achieved? What about wings? On our non-existent budget, could we do any of this without it looking faintly ridiculous? Getting the angel 'on' and 'off' was also

going to be difficult, as he appears to Mary in the middle of a street scene. The idea was that when the angel appeared, all activity on stage would freeze, leaving only Mary mobile and able to interact with him. When the angel exited, everyone would be reanimated, unaware of the experience Mary had had.

Our director came up with the solution – not only would the people in the street not see the angel, but neither would we. Only Mary would see the angel – after all, it's only her he's come to see.

The first time I saw this it was extremely effective. The naturalistic general lighting came down suddenly as Mary was caught in a sharp bright white light directly above her, while a carefully positioned wind machine blew her clothes and hair about, but left everyone else untouched. The visual effect was that Mary seemed caught up in her own personal and private storm. The only problem was that the wind machine was extremely noisy, considerably detracting from the atmosphere of the moment. This was solved by the sound engineer, who mixed together a howling gale, a heavenly choir, and a voice whispering 'Mary…' which covered the sound of the machine, while adding a new dimension to the effect. The combined effect of light, wind and sound remains extraordinary and magical and when the scene returns to 'normal' you have a very real sense that something has happened to Mary that she is unable to explain to anyone else. (The effect is repeated later when the shepherds see the angel, though it has a spookier feeling here as they are alone on a hillside in the middle of the night.)

Solving the angel problem proved the old saw that necessity is the mother of invention – practical and budgetary constraints, approached creatively, can actually lead to better effects and outcomes than what you would have done had you had more money.

For all the difficulties that working in Holy Trinity Church presented, it had the great advantage that its architecture gave us the basis of an authentic feeling set. The great stone columns and arches could suggest Herod's palace at one time or the backdrop to a street in Nazareth. We were usually rehearsing in the church in the evenings, so it was only when the director went into the church during the day on one occasion that he started to think about how to exploit the enormous colourful stained glass windows. The moment in the play when any sense of realism is elbowed out is at the very end, when the entire cast is assembled on stage to sing the *Hallelujah Chorus*. To make this finale really glorious, lights were fixed to the *outside* of the church, so that light shone in through the stained glass windows, illuminating them during this number. Again, this remains a wonderful effect and came out of using what was already there in an imaginative way.

So, special effects can be used to solve problems and also to enhance the peculiarities of your venue. They need not be complex or expensive (our wind machine is an agricultural fan, borrowed from a local farmer).

7. Administration

Most of this section deals with the least creatively inspiring – but nonetheless absolutely essential – aspects of mounting a community play: tasks which ideally should be tackled by someone with a flair for administration or someone used to dealing with health and safety issues. If you don't have an ideal volunteer, this section is designed for someone who has never undertaken this kind of role before.

The first thing to recognise is that these are all vital tasks – not only to guarantee, as far as possible, the safety and well-being of your participants and audience, but because most funding will depend on you having the following policies and procedures in place. Consequently, none of this can be left until the last minute and much of it needs to be completed in advance of submitting funding applications.

Risk assessment

Don't be daunted by the idea of a risk assessment if you haven't done one before. You probably naturally do risk assessments all the time without realising it. It's really a case of thinking about all the aspects of the production which could go wrong with serious consequences: 'What if…?' and working out how to reduce these risks (you can't eliminate all risk) and what you would do in the worst case scenario. It needn't be a case of 'health-and-safety-gone-mad' and should give you some peace of mind in the long run.

For example, our own play is preceded by Mary and Joseph and a donkey processing through the village, followed by all the children, setting off from the village school, calling at both village pubs and being turned away, before continuing on to the church where the performance proper takes place. While this is a charming prelude to the play, it is probably the most potentially hazardous activity it involves, and it is only by assessing all the possible dangers that it is rendered as safe as it can be.

Initially I thought the greatest risk was that the landlords of the two pubs (who had gamely agreed to co-operate in September) would forget, with the increased Christmas custom, that they were supposed to be available to tell Mary and Joseph that there was 'no room at the inn' (in fact, this has never been a problem; the most unexpected contribution being when one invited

them in for a drink). This of course was not actually a safety hazard and its priority in my mind at the time demonstrates how you can get tunnel vision. My biggest valid anxiety was having all those children walking in the road (the pavement is too narrow), in the dark, as there is a fairly busy crossroads just before they get to the church. The one hazard I had not thought about was the donkey.

Our next door neighbour happened to have the only two donkeys in the village, so borrowing one was negotiated. There was a 'bad' donkey, my neighbour told me, and a 'good' donkey, so it was a fairly easy choice. When I explained the procession to Mary and Joseph it became clear that Mary was frightened of all quadrupeds and extremely anxious about the whole enterprise. The first practice run with the donkey took place in the daytime, with Mary and Joseph in costume (we also wanted to get some photographs to use in publicity) and no children. On our way from the donkey's home to the point of assignation with Joseph and Mary, the donkey's owner mentioned that the donkey didn't like bright lights, didn't like the sensation that anyone was behind her and had a fear of drains. During our rather eccentric progress

(avoiding drains) I realised that this donkey was not going to cope with car headlights or chattering children following her. We reached the *rendez-vous* with Joseph and a white-faced Mary. The donkey was not keen on being led by Joseph and kept going towards its owner until we decided it was safer if she led the donkey and Joseph and Mary walked beside it. This worked well enough, though my growing sense that it was all going to be an utter disaster was confirmed when the donkey was led across the road to avoid one drain, only to find herself confronted with another on the other side, and backed up until she was in the middle of the crossroads having decided she was not going anywhere until all the drains went away.

As the traffic from all quarters built up while donkey-coaxing ensued and Mary whitened further, the impossibility of the whole thing was forcibly insisting itself on me. I was most worried that the donkey would suddenly bolt and everything had taken so much longer than anticipated that we were approaching coming-out-of-school time, which increased all hazards by an incalculable degree. The only thing which somewhat relieved the pressure was the motorists' patience and amusement at the spectacle of Joseph and the donkey owner wrestling with the donkey (the owner hissing, 'We can't *make* her; she has to *want* to do it,') while I comforted Mary, who looked on, hands to her mouth, in what must have seemed an over-theatrical expression of dismay at the scene. (I later discovered we sold tickets to a family from another village because the mother had witnessed this living drama on her way home from the supermarket.) The recalcitrant animal was eventually persuaded to resume progress, the photos were taken and my neighbour and I returned home with the donkey (avoiding drains by miles, now) discussing what could be done. 'I suppose we could try the *bad* donkey,' she said.

The bad donkey, it turned out, was a born trouper. Not only did he not mind Joseph leading him, nor children following him, nor cars, nor headlights, nor drains, but realising he was a star, he seemed to know when anyone was taking his photograph and stopped and posed. Even Mary stroked him. Quite why he was a bad donkey, we never found out. Perhaps he just *wanted* to do it.

I did not realise in the minutes that seemed hours stranded on the crossroads that we were actually doing a practical informal risk assessment.

The difference between this and doing a formal risk assessment was that we were learning ad hoc by experience, and while these are lessons you never forget, a formal risk assessment means you don't miss things you haven't even thought of.

A formal risk assessment assigns a level of *hazard* to anything which could cause *harm* – high, medium, or low. So, if you are putting on your play in a big top, the hazard level attached to the big top catching fire would be high, as if this actually happened it would be very dangerous. But it also assigns a level of *risk*, which is the *likelihood* of the big top catching fire in the first place. In this case the level would be low.

The point of the risk assessment is to (1) identify the hazards and calculate the risks and (2) take steps to reduce or eliminate the risks.

Sometimes the only way of reducing a risk is by making people aware that the hazard exists.

Your risk assessment should look at each element of an activity and ask:

- what is a potential problem and who is at risk?

- what would be the effect?

- what controls are in place?

- what risks are not controlled?

- what action is required?

- who is responsible?

Let's apply these considerations to the donkey on a public highway as a potential problem/hazard.

- The *effect* of him refusing to co-operate could lead to a traffic-jam and children standing in the road waiting, which could form a medium to high hazard. With the first donkey this would have been high risk (likely), with the second donkey it was low risk (unlikely), but because animals are unpredictable there will never be no risk at all.

- *Controls in place* are: an obedient donkey and a competent donkey handler with whom the donkey is familiar. (This makes it low risk as there is no stronger precaution you can take.)

- *Uncontrolled risks* include the donkey bolting due to an unforeseen event alarming it – an irate motorist sounding their horn, for example, or a screaming child. (I thought this was medium risk, but it has turned out to be low risk – the donkey has never bolted. Nevertheless it *could*.)

- *What action is required and who is responsible?* The donkey handler is ultimately responsible for the donkey. In the worst possible scenario, if the donkey bolts, it will be difficult to locate in the dark and could cause a hazard to traffic or injure itself. It is therefore wearing a fluorescent blanket and flashings on its hooves.

Let's now consider the potential risk to the children participating in a procession on a public highway. The hazards to the children are: traffic, darkness, stopping and starting, the possibility of the donkey bolting. If no account were taken of any of these factors, this would be a very high risk activity.

Controls in place are school staff and parent volunteers accompanying the children and the fact that the children know the route, and the rules, and have done it in daylight. (Rules include: keeping together, listening to instructions, not startling the donkey.) Accompanying adults are in high-visibility tabards, are at the front and back of the procession and dotted throughout it. Children are carrying lights. The local police have agreed to come and conduct the procession over the crossroads (by stopping the traffic) if they are available. School staff will follow their own procedure for safe crossing if no police are available.

These measures have considerably reduced all risks, leaving only the risk of the donkey bolting an uncontrollable one. In this event, adults accompanying the procession make sure the children remain in the group and resume the procession without the donkey when possible. (This is because, whatever happens, the children still need to be got safely to the church.)

A common sense mental walk through your event, taking into account all the 'what ifs...' is probably more efficiently done by a small group rather than one person, as different perspectives identify different risks and can also come up with a range of solutions. To do a risk assessment you need to think through not only the production itself and the risks entailed but the process of setting up and striking the set. Risking breaking the law is also a hazard, so you need to be aware of those you need to comply with.

Here are some aspects to consider including in your risk assessment (some will be irrelevant to you and there will be some relevant to you that are not on this list):

Access

Are your vehicles or those of the audience going to cause hazards for local residents? How are you going to ensure an ambulance or a fire engine can get the closest access? What arrangements are there for disabled people's access? What trip hazards are there? Are you complying with the law?

Alcohol

If alcohol is to be sold are you complying with the law? Is there likely to be drink consumed in public places? (Some places have by-laws prohibiting the consumption of alcohol in the street.) What happens if someone becomes drunk and disorderly – or just a nuisance? What are you doing to ensure there is no under-age drinking? What are you doing about responsibly disposing of bottles and cans?

Animals

Consider: their well-being (shade, water, food, security); the risk they pose to the public – and vice versa; the risk they pose to facilities; arrangements for accidents or illness; transportation.

Audience

Audience safety issues should be covered by other headings listed here, but try to 'walk through' (once well in advance, and again just before the event when new hazards may be in place) all the areas an audience member might use (including any bar/refreshment area/cloakrooms/toilets, especially if any of these are temporary structures, not usually on this site), from arriving at the venue to leaving it, and identify any worries.

Children

What isn't covered by your child protection policy? (The CPP is covered later in this section.) Who is responsible for first aid to children?

Communication

Do you need walkie-talkies for the production team? What are the procedures for transmitting messages, from a lost child to a security threat?

Electricity

Is the power supply suitable for your needs? Are both performers and audience safe from trip hazards caused by cables? Is there protection from sources of water? Is your emergency lighting a separate system and is it being regularly tested? What is the procedure in case of the power supply failing?

Emergency and Evacuation

What is the evacuation procedure (emergency exits and assembly points)? Who takes charge of calling for an evacuation and of supervising it? Who calls the emergency services? Who monitors the emergency?

Equipment

Consider its safety, its security and its storage when not in use.

Fire

What are the hazards? Consider whether flammable materials as well as mains gas, LPG, oil or petrol are present on site. Where are the fire exits and are they clear of obstructions and operational? Are they clearly marked and identifiable if the power is cut?

First aid

Who are your first-aiders and is their training up-to-date? Do they know where the first aid box is and is it fully stocked?

Performers

Are you using naked flames, and if so, what steps are you taking to minimise the risk to performers? (E.g. child + flammable costume + candle + excitement = unacceptable risk). If your performers have to lie on the ground or go in bare feet, what precautions are you taking to make sure the performance area is free of sharp objects? (Even if you sweep the area before the show, what happens if a glass or ceramic prop is broken onstage during the performance?) Are there trip hazards on the set which have to be navigated in blackout? How are you avoiding the creation of bottle-necks when a lot of people are going on or off stage at the same time (especially if there are steps)? Are there props and costumes which could be hazardous to the performers? (E.g. high heels + dancing or uneven surfaces = hazard; vigorous activity such as running in long costumes = hazard; voluminous sleeves/long scarves, skirts or trains that can catch or snag or be stepped on = hazard. All these hazards are increased if the performer is carrying something.) Consider your performers are of differing physical abilities – not everyone, for example, can get off the stage quickly in the dark and you need to make allowances for this. Have you got adequate insurance cover? (Insurance is covered later in this section.)

Public conveniences

Are there enough? Are they accessible? If they are hired 'portable' toilets, do you have to hand details of who you need to contact if they get blocked or overflow?

Security

What are the arrangements for handling cash for tickets and purchases and its security? What do performers do with their personal valuables during the performance?

Temporary structures

With tents/marquees watch out for guide ropes and for barricades, temporary tables (e.g. for box office or other sales), check that they are correctly positioned and not causing a hazard in themselves. Are they stable?

With newly erected signs: are they securely fixed and do they do the job?

With any kind of staging or platforms, check that it is safe and that hazards are minimized. Are performers familiar with the set and backstage area? Are they aware of hazards?

Are the public and performers to be excluded from the venue during construction and striking? Is it a hard-hat area? Is there sufficient insurance for these activities?

Traffic

Is your activity going to have an impact on road traffic? Have you sought the necessary permissions? If necessary, do you have separate safe pedestrian access?

Water

If your activity is near open water, what safety measures are in place?

Weather

Could extreme weather conditions adversely affect your event? How would you ameliorate these? Have you considered the necessity of cancelling the event? Does your insurance cover this eventuality?

What else?

What does your production involve on stage that could be risky? Real food (how safe is it to eat)? Liquids that could be spilt and slipped on? Unwieldy or flammable props? Go through the script looking for trouble.

Many of the hazards listed can be reduced by the judicious employment of stewards. If these can double as first-aiders, so much the better. Your stewards are the ones that provide first response to a hazard (whether this is

quickly and efficiently clearing up broken glass or helping people to the exits in the event of an evacuation). If they can also deal with someone fainting or cutting themselves this is a bonus. Stewards need to be sensible reliable people who are fully acquainted with your risk assessment and know what to do when something goes wrong and do it calmly. They need to be able to use initiative and common sense (e.g. see when audience are obstructing aisles or exits and deal with it courteously but effectively). They need to be equipped with a torch and to be easily identifiable (e.g. badge or marked clothing). Stewards need to know the position of fire extinguishers and first aid kit/s; audience, performers and production crew need to be made aware of the position of emergency/fire exits.

If five or more people are formally *employed*, any significant findings of the risk assessment must be recorded. Having done a risk assessment does not protect you from all dangers, but reduces the risk of an accident or other misfortune, and, if something does go wrong, it shows you have taken all possible steps to anticipate and eliminate risks. For anyone facing a claim or prosecution relating to health and safety, the difference between having and not having a written risk assessment may be significant.

If the arrangements for your production are unusually complex and involve a huge number of people, you might want to refine your risk assessment further, so you can assess risk at a glance. To do this, score a risk activity both for (a) hazard and (b) risk, following this guide:

1 = low

1.5 = low-medium

2 = medium

2.5 = medium-high

3 = high

You then add both scores together and divide by 2 to get the combination of severity and the likelihood of occurrence. So the big top catching fire scenario (high/3 hazard; low/1 likelihood) would be calculated as a medium/2.

However, I am tempted to suggest that when you are thinking about numbers rather than hazards and risks you are moving away from the realities of the situation and you may consequently concentrate on apparently big risks with the possibility that you may run out of time to address apparently small ones. One small trip hazard may end up tripping up lots of people or just one person who is already very frail: all hazards are hazards, and the big ones are the ones usually least likely to occur because people tend automatically to take precautions.

Also, resist, but try to understand unfounded safety objections. I was once involved in a non-professional production set in a Wild West saloon. The set extended into the auditorium, so the audience was seated at tables in the saloon and the back wall of the main set on the stage comprised the (stage) bar, with floor to ceiling shelving full of bottles and glasses. About a week before the show opened, the committee who ran the venue prohibited us from using real glass bottles or glasses. (As this production was a fundraiser for our main community play we had no money – or inclination on the grounds of aesthetics – to replace hundreds of glass items with plastic.)

After a lot of discussion it transpired that this was a house rule because the big event for which the building was used as a theatre was the annual pantomime, which had lots of children skipping about in bare feet. Any real glass had naturally been banned from the stage, but somehow this had found its way into the venue rules for everyone else using the stage. (Particularly aggravating in this case was that the *audience* were allowed real glasses from the real bar, and much of the action took place in amongst them.) Once we realised where the ban originated we were able to negotiate real glass, by assuring the committee there were no children or bare feet in the production and by signing a disclaimer by which we took full responsibility for any accidents that arose from using real glass. When health and safety objections are raised which seem ridiculous to you, try to understand where they are coming from and accept responsibility for the risk yourself, if you are sure it is an admissible one. Sorting out these issues earlier rather than later saves stress at the time you don't need it.

As I said at the beginning, don't be daunted by the risk assessment. No-one sets out to arrange things dangerously, and if you aimed to avoid all risks you probably wouldn't get out of bed, let alone put on a play. If it is any comfort,

we have had very few accidents or incidents in our community play – no injury has required the attention of a doctor, and almost all of them happened to actors (not audience) during late rehearsals of the first production, when the risk assessment was still on my 'to do' list. Both involved people falling over: on steps not marked with hazard tape and tripping over things during a total blackout. Of the two accidents that didn't happen to an actor, one occurred to our sound man, setting up for the first production, who sprained his ankle doing something he should have had help with. All of these minor injuries could have been avoided and since then we have no rehearsals on the stage until all hazards have been marked and shown to performers; we have no absolute blackouts if people are moving about; we *try* to have no-one working alone in the church, but this is not always possible. The risk assessment is now completed early and then run over again once the stage and equipment are in place. The other accident, which we couldn't have anticipated, happened to our director, when he stepped off the stage minutes before the first ever performance. He went straight through the iron gratings in the floor of the church (which, having been there for a hundred or so years, no-one had thought might choose this moment to break).

So, the long and the short of it is: get help with the risk assessment, get help with reducing potential hazards, and get on with the production. It's not as hard as it looks, you've got to do it, and you will, in the long run, sleep better.

Child Protection

No harm should come to any child in the course of a well-organised community play. Because it is a populous event, children are unlikely to be in a situation where an unsavoury adult can pose any risk to them in a solitary situation, and any real risks may well lie outside what you are able to control. As a matter of course, one person should be designated (perhaps the person generally 'in charge' of the children's contribution) to be responsible for seeing that children are collected after rehearsals and performances by an authorised person. (You can ask for this to be specified on the first contact with parents, on the 'permission to participate' form. Similarly the form can ask whether the child has parental permission to find their own way home.) This person needs to be able to wait until the last child is collected and have at all times a full list of contact details, so errant or forgetful parents can be chased. Because this person may be left alone with a child, they need to be Criminal Records Bureau (CRB) checked. CRB checking will crop up several times in this section – it can take time to complete so again this is a task which needs to be embarked on at the earliest stage. Enrolling the assistance of a teacher or classroom assistant or dinner lady or playground supervisor (all of whom will have been CRB checked) may be the path of least resistance.

If you are working closely with a school, their staff will of course have been checked with the CRB and will also be aware of the relevant issues through the school's own Child Protection Policy (CPP). Any other adults working closely or unsupervised with children must also be CRB checked and fully aware of the CPP. (I personally am checked for each production both by the village school and by the church.) Go to www.crb.gov.uk for details on how to effect a check. Despite this safeguard, national paranoia about child abuse had reached such a height by the last production that I asked – which I never had before – whether someone should be present in the room while I measured the children for their costumes. While this involves measuring them over their normal clothes, I wanted to at least register that I had been happy to have someone with me. (We all need to be prepared to confront uncomfortable issues and heightened sensitivity when it comes to child protection.) You need to assign someone to be Designated Person for Child Protection: these must be CRB checked and will ideally be: the person responsible for the children's input (who will be most familiar with each child's personal and family circumstances), a teacher, a youth worker, or a social worker.

As well as avoiding situations which could be misconstrued, adults working with children also have a moral responsibility not to ignore signs that a child may be being abused elsewhere (i.e. outside the activity of the community play). Your CPP should include these points, as well as clear guidelines on what to do if abuse is suspected or alleged. If you have any doubts about drawing up your own CPP, consult the NSPCC (email: info@nspcc.org.uk) or your local authority for guidance. The following 'model' CPP is the one we use. (We were unable to find a CPP for a community play, so in consultation with the participating school staff, developed and adapted a model policy for an after-school club to create this.)

**A model Child Protection Policy for a
Community Play Organisation**

[Name of Community Play Organisation] fully recognises the responsibility it has to have arrangements about safeguarding and promoting the welfare of children.

This document sets out how [Name of Community Play Organisation] will meet those responsibilities.

Hereafter, all adults working closely with children, whether paid or unpaid, are referred to as: 'staff'.

If a child is being abused

Staff can have an important role to play in noticing indicators of possible abuse or neglect though their contact with children. It is important that all staff know what to do if they have any such concerns. See Appendix 2 for a list of contact details for any authorities mentioned.

- Staff will create and maintain an ethos where children are encouraged to talk and are listened to.

- Staff will have an awareness of the indicators of abuse and always take any concerns seriously.

- If staff have any suspicion that a child is being abused they will report this to Children's Social Care Services or the Police Child and Domestic Abuse Central Referral and Tasking Unit. See Appendix 1 for categories of abuse. If staff have any doubts about the appropriateness of a child protection referral they will take further advice from the Designated Person for Child Protection.

- If a child discloses that s/he has been abused, staff cannot promise a child that this will be kept a secret.

Code of conduct for staff

- Staff are responsible for their own actions and behaviour and should avoid any contact which would lead any reasonable person to question their motivation and intentions.

- Staff will ensure their behaviour remains professional at all times, including their use of language.

- Physical contact between staff and children should be limited to what is required for the purposes of the play. Younger children may generally need more personal contact than older children. Adults should avoid any physical contact which could be misconstrued.

- Staff should avoid working in one-to-one situations with children but where this is necessary they should ensure there is visual access and remote or secluded areas should be avoided. (E.g. if you are alone with a child, always leave the door open.)

- Staff will never allow or condone bullying or threatening behaviour by adults or children, whether physical or verbal.

- Adults should not transport children in their cars without the express agreement of parents except in case of emergency.

Preventing unsuitable persons from working with children

Where staff are paid employees of [Name of Community Play Organisation]:

The [Name of Community Play Organisation]will operate safe recruitment practices including ensuring appropriate CRB checks and references are taken up. Referees will be asked whether they have any reason to doubt the suitability to work with children.

Where staff are volunteers:

The [Name of Community Play Organisation] will ensure that CRB checks are in place for any adults working closely and/or unsupervised with children.

The Designated Person for Child Protection will consult with the Manager of the Child Protection Review Unit in the event of an allegation being made against an adult working in the [Name of Community Play Organisation]. S/he will adhere to the relevant procedures.

Appendix 1: The four categories of abuse

Physical abuse includes hitting, shaking, throwing, poisoning, burning/scalding, drowning, suffocating and fictitious or induced illness.

Neglect may involve persistent failure to

- provide adequate food, shelter and/or clothing

- protect a child from physical harm or danger

- ensure access to appropriate medical care or treatment

Emotional abuse is the persistent emotional/psychological ill treatment so as to cause severe and adverse effects on the child's emotional /psychological development. Some level of emotional abuse is present in all types of ill treatment although it may occur alone.

Sexual abuse involves forcing or enticing a child or young person to take part in sexual activities – whether or not the child is aware of what is happening. It may include physical contact including penetrative acts or non-penetrative acts, such as looking at or producing pornographic material, watching sexual activity, or encouraging children to behave in sexually inappropriate ways.

Appendix 2: Useful contacts

Designated Child Protection Person for [name of Community Play Association]

[Add name and telephone number]

Social Care Team [add telephone number]

Child Protection Review Manager [add telephone number]

Police – Child and Domestic Abuse Central Referral and Tasking Unit [add telephone number]

National Society for the Prevention of Cruelty to Children NSPCC 0808 800 5000 [end of Child Protection Policy]

Due to the unique nature of a community play, any children involved will necessarily be rehearsing and performing with adults who cannot *all* be CRB checked. On the other hand, CRB checks are not infallible and there is a first time for every child-abuser. The safest approach is to ensure no adult is alone with any child who they might not normally be alone with – e.g. their parent, their teacher, a trusted neighbour or friend's parent who often looks after them. Also, trust your instincts, as it is always better to be safe than sorry. If you feel uncomfortable about the behaviour of any adult, but cannot pin down the nature of your disquiet, just keep children away from them, without making it an issue and remain vigilant (as, indeed, you would in normal everyday life). As long as the CPP and these simple and common sense safeguards are in place, you have done all you can to ensure both children and adults can relax and enjoy working and playing together. (By way of reassurance: we have never had to refer to our CPP policy, as there has never been a problem of this nature. But it is vital to have it in place.)

Equal Opportunities

Although not required by law, it is generally considered good practice for organisations to have an Equal Opportunities Policy to show that they are actively opposing discrimination and that the opportunities they offer are available to everyone. Because the very nature of a community play defines it as an open and widely accessible project, and these values will be embedded in your constitution (see next item), an EOP may not seem necessary. However, an EOP is a requirement of many funding bodies, especially when the grant comes from public money. You can write your own, or adapt it from a model. If you prefer short and sweet, this is what we use:

A brief, simple model Equal Opportunities Policy for a Community Play

[Name of Community Play Association] recognises, and is opposed to, the fact that certain people are discriminated against, and undertakes to treat all equally, regardless of gender, sexual orientation, age, race, nationality, religion, mental or physical health or ability.

By advertising its activities throughout the community and strenuous efforts to encourage participation (either as performers or as spectators) from all quarters, [Name of Community Play Association] aims to represent the community in all its diversity.

[Name of Community Play Association] will monitor the profile of those engaging in its activities in order to uphold these values.

You can go into a lot more detail, if you feel it is appropriate to your group, and if you have the resources to do so, for example, about: providing your publicity material in Braille, on tape, in large format or in other languages when requested; providing signers or interpreters; ensuring any images you use for publicity are inclusive; making rehearsal and performance venues more accessible to those with disabilities; having representation from different groups on the decision-making/production team; detailing how you are monitoring and evaluating breadth of participation; procedures for dealing with discrimination if it occurs.

If you are formally employing staff you will need to conform with anti-discrimination legislation and include a recruitment and employment procedure in your policy. This is an area too complex to enter into here and you need to seek further information.

(See www.direct.gov.uk/en/employment)

Constitution

Most funders will want to see your group's Constitution. This again need not be complicated. It should contain:

The name of the group as it appears on your bank account.

Objectives of the group: a brief comprehensive statement will do.

Powers: how the group will achieve its objectives.

Committee: how the core group is elected or appointed. The constitution should state there are at least three people in this management committee. This could be your director, your producer and your treasurer, or any other grouping that can lead decision making.

Membership: how people can join your group.

Payments or benefits: public funders will need to see there is no private gain or profit, i.e. no-one makes money from the organisation, such as through a dividend or bonus. This excludes reasonable expenses and paying staff.

Closing down/dissolution clause: what happens to any assets if/when the group is wound up.

Adopting the constitution

Your group's management committee needs to discuss and agree the constitution, sign and date it.

A model constitution for a Community Play Association mounting a one-off production

[Name of Community Play Association] exists to facilitate the mounting of a large-scale community play on… [Add dates. If you don't have fixed dates yet, the month or even season and year will do.]

By involving a range of local organisations and many more local individual citizens, the organisation aims to include anyone and everyone who feels they have something to offer the project.

[If your organising/management committee has been elected, say when and how. If, however, it is largely self-appointed/informally recruited, you can say something like this:] The core of organisers have co-operated as a facilitating body to enable the broadest possible participation in the project. We have had no elections, as [Name of Community Play Association] has been set up by liaising with existing community groups in order to mount a single production. This is a group established for a one-off theatrical and social experience and we have consequently approached established and experienced local professionals and community leaders to form our committee, in order to provide a balance of professional expertise and local knowledge and contact-bases.

The group is open to everyone in the community and its activities are being widely publicised; indeed strenuous efforts are being made to reach those whom existing local groups often fail to involve.

No individual will profit from the production, although some aspects of the production, such as professional lighting and sound, will be paid for. When the group is disbanded, following the production, any assets would be distributed to local projects of an associated nature; however, it is not anticipated that there will be any assets.

The group has existed informally since [insert date]. This constitution was officially adopted on [insert date].

Witnessed by:

[e.g.] Chair [insert name, signature and date]

[e.g.] Convenor [insert name, signature and date]

[e.g.] Secretary [insert name, signature and date]

If you find that your community play association wants to continue to put on plays, you will need to revise your constitution accordingly.

A model constitution for a Community Play Association intending regularly to produce community plays

[Name of Community Play Association] exists to provide the opportunity for local people to be involved in musical and theatrical productions of a professional standard and for the local community to have access to performances of this calibre as audiences. Open to everyone, [Name of Community Play Association]'s principal priority is regularly to mount a large scale community play.

The whole group, which remains a non-profit-making organisation, will meet formally once a year to review democratically the structure of the committee, elect representatives and to plan the year ahead. Other administrative or business meetings will be held ad hoc, according to the demands and hierarchy of the project in hand.

The preferred make-up of the committee consists of Convenor/Chair, Secretary, Treasurer, Artistic Director, Band representative, Choir representative, Church representative, School representative.

In the event of the organisation being disbanded, a vote would be taken by all members attending an E.G.M. on which charitable association would receive any remaining assets.

This revised constitution was adopted at the A.G.M. on [insert date].

Witnessed by:

[e.g.] Artistic Director [insert name, signature and date]

[e.g.] Convenor [insert name, signature and date]

[e.g.] Secretary [insert name, signature and date]

Insurance

First of all, check what insurance is already in place. Performance venues will almost certainly have their own insurance, but check what is actually covered and whether you are engaging in activities excluded from their insurance. Similarly, contractors you hire in (lighting and sound services, for example) will have their own insurance, but again check what is covered.

If you employ staff you are required by law to have *Employer's Liability Insurance*. This covers your employees in the event of an accident, disease or injury caused or worsened by work undertaken for you. It is a moot point whether volunteers are 'employees', but they have been considered so in some industrial tribunals.

You will definitely need *Public Liability Insurance*. Don't assume that because your venue has this, you are covered. For example, the church we use for our play has this cover, but it extends only to activities normally undertaken in the building and we have to take out our own, separate, cover for the duration of the play.

You may wish to include *Property Cover* (again, expensive items such as lighting and stage equipment are likely to be covered by the companies you are hiring from, but do check) and also *Cancellation Cover*, which recompenses you in the event that you cannot go ahead with the production.

Your best bet is to go to a broker who specialises in 'event' insurance as they will be aware of the kinds of activities you want to insure. They will want to know, apart from the general 'where, what and when' details, the maximum number of people attending – remember *this must include your performers* as well as your anticipated audience.

Make sure you disclose all the facts accurately, that you read the small print, and particularly the exclusions. Keep two copies of the policy in separate locations, in the event of flood damage or fire.

Monitoring and evaluation

Monitoring and evaluation are things you need to bear in mind even if you have no intention of mounting a similar event in the future. Firstly, you may change your mind about doing it, or something similar, again, and having kept a record of the event will prove invaluable if you do; secondly, funders often require a post-event report. Monitoring in this context is generally checking you are where you planned to be at any stage. (If, for example, you find that crowd scenes are taking a lot more time to rehearse than you had anticipated and allowed for, you can slot in extra rehearsals, but knowing this will also help you when planning a rehearsal schedule in the future.) Evaluation involves assessing the project's successes and failings once it's over. Making a note of what went wrong, what could have been better organized, where time/resources could have been saved is also extremely useful. *You* will know to what extent you achieved what you set out to do, and in some cases you may have exceeded expectation, or there may have been unexpected (bonus) positive outcomes, and this is all worth recording.

You also ought to get retrospective feedback from participants and audience members. Ideally, leave a brief questionnaire or feedback card on each seat, or have someone interview people randomly as they leave. A long detailed questionnaire asking questions of ethnicity and age-group is unlikely to get many respondents from people anxious to get home, but these are questions you can ask participants to answer during the rehearsal process. A card left on each seat asking for audience members' comments on the production is easy both for you to organize and for them to comply with. (You can easily sneak in: 'if you would like to be kept informed of other events from Ourtown Community Play Association, please give your name and postal/email address' and you have the beginnings of a supporters' database.) As soon as possible after the last night also invite feedback from participants. This can be a general question which they can answer however they like, or a more formal questionnaire which, if sent by email, is easy to fill in and makes it easy to chase up procrastinators. Again, this not only helps you evaluate how well things worked from their perspective, but gives you the kind of 'proof' funders are looking for to justify their investment. Funders and similar bodies gain confidence from you using their language but you don't want to inflict the jargon on everyone else, so here is a breakdown/translation of the kinds of questions you should be asking yourself and others:

Baseline: What exists at the start of a project. This can help show gaps in provision or prove the need for the project to happen.

Demographics: Details such as age, sex, ethnicity and place of birth of people involved (as spectators and participants).

Inputs: Time, money and resources that go into the running of the project.

Outcomes: Changes that the project has made to the group or community. These can include increased skills, confidence and knowledge amongst the people in the group.

Outputs: Measurable evidence about what happened as a result of the project. They show how close to your original targets you were. For example, if you set out to do workshops with twenty young people, what numbers did you actually get?

Quantitative or 'hard' data: This is the numbers bit – i.e. figures that show what happened during a project. You can find out how many people participated, of what age, where from, what they liked/disliked, what they spent money on etc. Statistics like these help you identify an audience profile that can show up gaps in provision as well as new opportunities. This 'measurable' data is collected through ticket sales, tick box forms, clickers and other methods.

Qualitative or 'soft' data: This shows people's experience of the project, including the audience, participants, artists and organisers. Although it isn't 'measurable' data, it can reveal the impact a project has on people's lives or on the local community. Did people learn new skills, gain confidence or make new friends? Has the project made the community feel closer? Information can be gathered through photos, video and talking to people in an informal way.

Performance Indicators: these are highlights that happen throughout a project, indicating points in time or achievements. Having a number throughout the life of a project helps you measure that you are on course for achieving your goal.

Target Group: the main group or groups you are working with and the people your activity, service or event is for. Your project will probably attract different kinds of people but it is important to be clear about the people who are most likely to participate in your activity. Which groups will benefit or change as a result of the project?

In my experience, in a low budget production there is very little time and fewer resources for this level of monitoring and evaluation. We tend to confine our efforts to recording the demographic of our participants and soliciting 'soft' data in the form of a short, simple 'open' questionnaire after the production (which also includes a question on what could have been done better); we also collect and archive all unsolicited feedback from audiences. These basic methods have proved adequate and useful for feedback to funders, for subsequent applications for funding, and for our own good practice.

8. Publicity

This subject has already been covered to some extent in the section on recruiting participants, and publicity to attract an audience should build on the media relationships established at that stage.

Compile a Mailing List

Using all the email addresses of everyone involved in the production as well as those who have helped or supported in some way, compile an alphabetical list which can be used to send out e-flyers in advance of the performance dates. This will generate ticket sales.

In addition, compile a list of addresses of those who don't have email and send them printed flyers at least three weeks in advance of the performance dates to allow people time to put the dates in their diary. This list should also be prepared well in advance with the contact details of any press or media people you wish to target with your publicity information and Press Release.

Writing a Press Release

Your basic Press Release needs to be strong, clear and appealing. It's very easy for press releases to meander off the point (especially if you are closely involved with the project) so keep it relatively short and sweet and get fresh eyes to look it over. Some journalists will use the press release to fill in details in their own stories, others are not above concocting a story purely out of information you supply – either way you want to make your story stand out from others they may be considering.

Try to make sure your press release includes answers to the following questions:

- what is it? – the central idea, first – enlarge later.

- when is it?

- where is it?

- why is it being done, now?

- who is involved?

- what makes it special? (i.e. one-off, scale, spectacular, unique, etc.)

- how is it different from other things people are likely to see/have seen?

- to whom will it appeal?

- what known credentials have been brought to bear on the project? (e.g. funding, 'names' involved or supporting)

Also include some useful 'quotations' – from the director, the writer, community leaders who are involved – and a contact number and email address from where journalists can get further information, arrange interviews, etc. Most importantly, credit your financial supporters and add the logos of any company or institution that has provided funding or sponsorship for the production.

A picture is worth a thousand words, as they say, and having photographs to go with the story will be essential. Local press photographers tend to turn up at inconvenient times, often during later rehearsals, when you really won't want to stop while they arrange the scene to suit the picture they want to take.

The Haddenham
Nativity 2009

Holy Trinity Church
Haddenham
10th, 11th, 12th December
7:30pm

Tickets £5 adults, £2.50 children
Available from Haddenham Galleries, Spar & Post Office
Or contact mail@community-play.org

This can be avoided by having a costumed rehearsal as soon as enough lighting is up to show things off to their best advantage and using your own photographer (your cast is bound to contain a talented amateur or two, if not professionals – or people who will recruit one) who can move about the set while you work, capturing the images which you feel are most striking. You can then select a few of the best and submit them to local newspapers with details of who and what they represent together with the press release. This then means that if and when a newspaper photographer does show up, you can explain they will have to shoot while the rehearsal is in progress, as they will already have a respectable number of images you are happy with. (You may well not want the kind of image they will tend to produce if they are allowed to get the actors to pose.)

Include photographs with your press release to help generate media interest. Make sure that you have permission from the photographer before reproducing any of his/her images in your publicity material and offering them for use by others.

Once you have your press release, send it by email to the arts desk of your local paper, and the editors of any local magazines. You can also try and send it to a named presenter or programme editor at your local radio station to try and get either an interview or a mention. If you are performing a publicity stunt which is visual, such as leading a donkey around the village, an email and follow-up phone call to your local TV news station may be worth trying.

Posters and flyers

Posters are worth spending good money on. If you don't have a budget for full colour, make sure your design is striking. Your cast may well contain someone who designs this kind of things for a living – make an appeal early for a designer. If you have developed a logo for the group or project this also needs to go on everything. Funders will also want their logos incorporated in any publicity material. Personal approaches about whether you can put them up are best – house-holders with prominent windows on busy streets are worth asking as is any shop or 'leisure' centre (e.g. swimming pool, pub, café, theatre, cinema). Have Blu-tack or Sellotape with you to make it easy for them to say 'yes'. Don't forget parish and village noticeboards.

Flyers can be adapted by simplifying the information on your poster. These can be delivered door-to-door, distributed with the local free paper, or bundles left at the till in shops, libraries, galleries, etc. where people can pick them up. If you have cultivated friendly shop-keepers, ask them to put one in every bag when they serve customers. A very effective method is to ask other local groups engaged in related activities whether you may hand them out, or place them on seats, at their performances and events leading up to yours. Ask everyone involved in the play to distribute leaflets to their friends, neighbours and colleagues. It doesn't matter if one household re-ceives three flyers by different means – this only emphasises the message. You can't have too many flyers.

Advertising

If you can afford advertising, target it. What does your audience read? Is there a local free paper? Again, don't forget parish magazines and local newsletters – they reach a lot of people in a specific area and (a) advertising here is cheap (you may even get it free) and (b) they may be very likely to use the 'story' in your press release.

Targeted email is perhaps the cheapest form of letting people know what you are doing. Including an image makes it more striking (but not one that takes ages to send or receive, the file size should be no more than around 150kB per email) and brief, sharp copy may distinguish it from other unsolicited mail and prevent it going straight in the trash. Include the name of the place your play is based in the subject line so people know it isn't random junk mail. (If you have a website, include the address in this and all other publicity.) Sending a publicity email to related or involved organisations and asking them to circulate it to their membership can reach a lot of people, and if you include a request to 'please forward this to anyone you think it may interest' can make it reach many more. Asking the cast to forward this email may also pay dividends, and they may well be more likely to do this than write to their friends saying 'please come and see me in our play'.

Social Media

It's becoming increasingly common for people to contact each other and arrange meetings via social media sites such as Facebook. You can set up your own Facebook site in the name of your community play and attract followers. This is where you can put up photos or even video clips of the production and invite feedback. And, essentially, you can keep people up-to-date about times and dates, venues, ticket prices and contact details should they wish to attend or get involved.

Finally, 'talk up' the production wherever you go and to whoever you meet. If you (and other people) seem excited about the play, it makes an impression. Don't just tell people about the play, *invite* them. Even if they're not involved in the production, it's *their* community, and therefore *their* play.

Useful Contacts

For information on community theatre

www.theatreodyssey.com
www.islingtoncommunitytheatre.com
www.lincolncommunityplay.org.uk
www.londonbubble.org.uk
www.dorchestercommunityplay.org.uk
www.acta.f2s.com
www.valleytheatre.co.uk
www.alsagercommunitytheatre.org.uk
www.botleytheatre.co.uk
www.creditonartscentre.org
Woking Community Play Association: enquiries@thevision.org.uk

For advice on funding

Arts Council
Website: www.artscouncil.org.uk
Tel: 0845 3006200
Fax: 0161 934 4426

For general theatrical enquiries

Equity
Website: www.equity.org.uk
Tel: 020 7670 0240 (general enquiries)

Director's Guild of Great Britain
Website: www.dggb.co.uk
Email: info@dggb.org
Tel: 020 8871 1660

Writer's Guild of Great Britain
Website: www.writersguild.org.uk
Email: erik@writersguild.org.uk
Tel: 020 7833 0777

Independent Theatre Council (I.T.C)
Website: www.itc-arts.org
Email: admin@itc-arts.org
Tel: 020 7089 6821 (admin)

The Stage
Website: www.thestage.co.uk
Email: gen_enquiries@thestage.co.uk
Tel: 020 7403 1818

Costume and props hire

Surrey Arts Wardrobe
Tel: 01483 721697
Email: sa.wardrobe@surreycc.gov.uk

National Theatre
Website: www.nationaltheatre.org.uk
Costume
Tel: 020 7735 4774
Email: costume_hire@nationaltheatre.org.uk
Props
Tel: 020 7820 1358
Email: props_hire@nationaltheatre.org.uk

www.entsweb.co.uk/suppliers/costume
www.costumehire.co.uk
www.keeleyhire.co.uk

Lighting hire

www.trafalgarlighting.co.uk
www.impactproductions.co.uk
www.partylights.co.uk
www.pslx.co.uk
www.10outof10.co.uk
www.eventsolutions.co.uk

Bibliography

Balfour, Michael, *Theatre in Prison: theory and practise* (Intellect, 2004).

Basom, Jonas, 'The Benefits of Drama Education', The Drama Game File, www.dramaed.net/benefits.pdf (2005)

Fearnow, Mark, *Theatre and the good: the value of collaborative play* (Cambria Press, 2007).

'How children, adults and communities benefit from choruses: The Chorus Impact Study', www.chorusamerica.org/about_choralsinging.cfm (2009)

Potera, Carol, 'Acting Your Age', www.medicinenet.com/script/main/art.asp?articlekey=51488 (July 17th 2000).

Reay, Barry 'Popular Religion', in ed. Barry Reay, *Popular Culture in Seventeenth-Century England* (Croom Helm, 1985).

Reid, Fiona, 'Nowhere to go for Christmas', *BBC History Magazine*, *V*ol. 11, No. 13, Christmas 2010.

Thomson, James, 'From the Stocks to the Stage: Prison Theatre and the Theatre of Prison', in ed. Balfour, *Theatre in Prison*.

Welch, Graham, 'Yes we can!', www.singup.org/magazine/magazine-article/view/102-yes-we-can (2010)

www.tourismnortheast.co.uk – an excellent source of information and advice on organizing and publicising large events. Much of the advice on administrative aspects is used with their creators' permission.

aurora metro press

Founded in 1989 to publish and promote new writing, the company has specialised in new drama and fiction, winning recognition and awards from the industry.

Other books on theatre

A GUIDE TO UK THEATRE FOR YOUNG AUDIENCES
ed. Paul Harman

The quality and range of Theatre for Children and Young People in the UK is one of our greatest cultural assets. This essential book provides the first ever guide to the wealth of talent and creativity displayed by over 150 professional companies involved in theatre for young audiences. A lively and comprehensive overview of many of the best shows currently on offer for international touring.

~ An ideal resource for anyone interested in theatre for young audiences.
~ Full colour with many photographs from the shows.
~ Useful sections on funding and organisations.
~ Listings of hundreds of theatre companies in the UK.
~ Overview of the sector and information about touring.

£7.99
ISBN 978-19065820-9-8
104 pages pbk

www.aurorametro.com

ART, THEATRE AND WOMEN'S SUFFRAGE

Irene Cockroft and Susan Croft

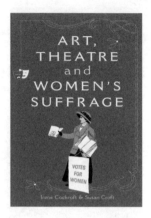

An exploration of the creative explosion that occurred when the campaign for the vote brought together the talents of so many female writers and artists at the start of the 20th century.

An overview of the artists, designers, writers and actors involved in the long campaign for women's suffrage.

Writers and artists including:

Cicely Hamilton/Chris St. John/Inez Bensusan/Elizabeth Robins/ Ernestine Mills/Pamela Colman Smith/Mary Lowndes/Emily Ford

£7.99
ISBN 978-1-906582-08-1
96 pages pbk

www.aurorametro.com